Inspirational Thoughts

of

Bishop Ezekiel Iyeke

Book I

Cover design by: Lisa Bracken Korloki Publishing Company
Interior design: Korloki Publishing Company
Summary: Religion and Self-Help

ISBN-13: 978-1936739318
ISBN-10: 1936739313

For additional copies of this or other Bishop Ezekiel Iyeke titles write:

Korloki Publishing Company

P.O. Box 300605 | Brooklyn NY 11230

Please allow 4 to 6 weeks for delivery.

For bulk orders contact us via email @ info@kpcbooks.com

PRINTED IN USA

Contents

Foreword

Chapter One: The Power to Prosper, **1**

Chapter Two: Attack the spirit of Jezebel, **21**

Chapter Three: Holy troublemakers, **41**

Chapter Four: I need a miracle, **59**

Chapter Five: How to maintain your Miracle, **79**

Chapter Six: The heavens becomes brass, **96**

Chapter Seven: Wrestling with shadows, **117**

Chapter Eight: Inspirational thoughts, **137**

Chapter Nine: The Appointed Time, **147**

FOREWORD

And there appeared a great wonder in heaven; a woman clothed with the sun, and the moon under her feet, and upon her head a crown of twelve stars: And she being with child cried, travailing in birth, and pained to be delivered.

And there appeared another wonder in heaven; and behold a great red dragon, having seven heads and ten horns, and seven crowns upon his heads. And his tail drew the third part of the stars of heaven, and did cast them to the earth: and the dragon stood before the woman who was ready to be delivered, for to devour her child as soon as it was born." (Revelation 12:1-4)

There is no gainsaying the fact that we struggle and labor to achieve and attain in life against the threat of constant obstacles and challenges that beset us round. Many times these can be resolved into physical factors as in conditions, situations and circumstances which may respond to a variety of remedies and solutions applied in a studied, deliberate manner over a period of time.

There are also, unfortunately, those situations that defy physical remedies. There are those cul-de-sacs, those dead-end situations in our lives, that defy all attempts toward resolution. Besides the physical and spiritual trauma they create in our lives, the mere fact of their existence and the dead-locked nature of their manifestation and occurrence in our lives itself creates a debilitation that erodes and wears heavy on our psyche and our morale. Many people have given up under these circumstances and resigned themselves to fate, others have taken matters into their own hands and ended their lives prematurely, or the lives of others whom they viewed as the threat to their peace and security.

Finally, there are those who are in dire physical and/or spiritual straits but do not even realize it, being effectively dead while they yet live. Many die on account of what is described as a "freak accident" -- in many instances they were already dead and it was only a matter of time before Satan showed up and made his collection.

Deliverance is an absolute necessity. Deliverance is an ongoing process that should be wrought in the life of the believer first at the personal level and then at other levels involving third or fourth parties as occasion demands. Our Lord said in Matthew 18:19: "That if two of you shall agree on earth as touching anything that they shall ask, it shall be done for them of my Father which is in heaven." In the immediate preceding verse our Lord also said: "Verily I say unto you, whatsoever ye shall bind on earth shall be bound in heaven: and whatsoever ye shall loose on earth shall be loosed in heaven." So, there things that need to be loosed on the earth (i.e. in your life and mine) that must first be loosed in heaven and there are things that must be bound on earth (i.e. your life and mine) that must first be bound in heaven.

In the Scripture verse from Revelation above, we are told about the great spiritual wonder or mystery in heaven where the woman (representing the Church) is clothed with the sun and the moon under her feet (i.e. the Church is clothed with the panoply and favor of the Sun of Righteousness, our Lord Jesus) and upon her head a crown of twelve stars (another symbol pointing to the spiritual authority of the Church), but despite all these accoutrements of divine office we are told that the woman is travailing with child (i.e. the purpose and destiny of God for the Church is straining to come to fruition and manifestation) "and pained to be delivered."

And why was the woman in so much pain only in the attempt to live out her dreams and fulfill her life's destiny (as so many of us want to do). The answer is given in the following verses:

"And there appeared another wonder in heaven; and behold a great red dragon, having seven heads and ten horns, and seven crowns upon his heads. And his tail drew the third part of the stars of heaven, and did cast them to the earth: and the dragon stood before the woman which was ready to be delivered, for to devour her child as soon as it was born."

Satan was standing by and creating the atmosphere that was designed to cause the woman's child (i.e. God's purpose) to be still-born. To kill the purpose of God in your life. To negate the purpose of God in your life. This is why deliverance is necessary. Notice the word is used repeatedly in those verses:

"travailing in birth, and pained to be **delivered***."*.... *"And the dragon stood before the woman which was ready to be* **delivered***, for to devour her child as soon as it was born."*

Deliverance is a necessity to give life and give full effect and complement to the purpose of God in your life and mine. Without the purpose of God being manifested in our lives Satan will not be cast out of the heaven from whence he stands as our accuser and that of our brethren. See the following verses of that Scripture in Revelation that talk about what happened and what will happen to you and I when God's purpose is fully born and realized in our lives.

"And she brought forth a man child, who was to rule all nations with a rod of iron: and her child was caught up unto God, and to his throne.

And there was war in heaven: Michael and his angels fought against the dragon; and the dragon fought and his angels, and prevailed not; neither was their place found any more in heaven. And the great dragon was cast out, that old serpent, called the Devil, and Satan, which deceiveth the whole world:

he was cast out into the earth, and his angels were cast out with him. And I heard a loud voice saying in heaven, now is come salvation, and strength, and the kingdom of our God, and the power of his Christ: for the accuser of our brethren is cast down, which accused them before our God day and night. And they overcame him by the blood of the Lamb and by the word of their testimony; and they loved not their lives unto the death." (Revelation 12:5-11)

This is why our Lord taught us to pray:

"...Our Father who art in Heaven, hallowed be thy name. Thy Kingdom come. **Thy will be done in my life as it is in heaven***."*

This is also why this book has been written. It is a manual, a guide, and an inspirational tool for believers to take charge of their own destiny and fulfill the Lord's will when He said:

"...Upon this Rock I will build my Church (i.e. the woman clothed with the sun), and the gates of hell shall not prevail against it (i.e. the great red dragon shall be cast out of the heaven where he stands to obstruct the purpose of God in our lives)."

Bishop Ezekiel Iyeke has been used by God in the area of deliverance for many years. With his experience and the inspiration of the Holy Spirit he has eloquently set forth this user guide as an effective tool for administering self-deliverance and deliverance to others as directed by the Spirit.

I recommend this book to all who earnestly search for a way out – either for themselves or for some other loved one. I encourage you to read it prayerfully and free from distractions and allow the Spirit of God to minister to you in the precise area of your need. As you do this, God will richly bless and empower you.

The grace of our Lord Jesus Christ is with you.

Prophet Kevin Etta
-Author of Dreams and Visions

Chapter One

Power to Prosper

"But thou shall remember the Lord thy God: for it is he that giveth thee power to get wealth that he may establish his covenant which he swore unto thy fathers, as it is this day." Deuteronomy 8:18:

In the foregoing, the Bible talks about power to prosper. It is a good thing to talk about prosperity and to preach about it. But the subject of prosperity must be balanced with the subject of holiness so that after we have prospered, we would not go to hell fire.

Psalm 84:11 says, "For the Lord God is a sun and shield; the Lord will give grace and glory: no good thing will he withhold from them that walk uprightly." Our God is clothed in glory and there is no reason why His children should wear rags; it does not make sense. Psalm 24:1 says, "The earth is the Lord's and the fullness thereof: the world and they that dwell therein." If God owns the earth and the fullness thereof, and I am His son, I must prosper. All the money in the world belongs to our heavenly Father. If you don't have your own share of it now, perhaps somebody is keeping it for you, waiting for you to grow up before handing it over to you. But you will surely get it. The time has actually come for unbelievers to be removed from the positions of power, so that the gospel can prosper. Allowing them to be in control of the economy would certainly hinder the course of the gospel.

There are many people that have the keys of poverty in their hands and until they drop them, there is absolutely nothing God can do to help them. God has so designed His plans that He places first things first. A lot of people claim that Abraham's blessings are theirs, the question is, will they allow God to run them through what He made Abraham to go through? Abraham first became a friend of God. He was righteous, he had faith and then God blessed him. Nowadays, people want to do it the other way round. They want money first. They want to be comfortable first before they serve the Lord.

Unfortunately, it does not work that way. Anybody that cannot serve the Lord when he or she is poor will not be able to serve Him when he or she gets rich.

Let us look at the twenty keys of poverty. If you have these keys in your hands, you need to pray hard to drop them so that you do not labor in vain. Sometimes, what you think is a big problem is a small one. You must have sweated before discovering that it was just a simple thing you needed to drop for your life to be overflowing with blessings.

Twenty Keys of Poverty

Stinginess: Proverbs 11: 24 says, "There is that scattereth, and yet increaseth; and there is that withholdeth more than is meet, but it tendeth to poverty."

Stinginess leads to poverty. This is where God's mathematics is different from our own mathematics. It is more logical to keep money, hoard it, or pile it up to become rich. But God's law says that he that scatters increases, but he that withholds, gets poor.

A certain man was on a salary of Five hundred dollar and was paying Fifty dollar as tithe per month. After some time, God blessed him and he started earning Five thousand dollar per month and as such, he had to pay Five hundred dollar for tithe every month. This man went to the pastor and said he needed counseling. The pastor asked him why he needed counseling and he said that five hundred dollar was too much for him to pay as tithe every month because he felt that it could buy so many things.

The pastor said, "No problem sir, let me pray that God should return you to your former income so that you will be able to pay fifty dollar which you can afford." A lot of Christians treat God as if He is an errand boy who they give tips. God is not also a beggar. He does not need your alms. If you are reading this message and you are still stingy, stop it because the Bible says that a stingy person is cursed. The key to receiving is giving. Anyone who does not give is like a Dead Sea. The problem of a Dead Sea is that it does not give out, it keeps everything inside and so, it stinks because it is not refreshed.

Loving sleep: Proverb 20: 13 says, "Love not sleep, lest thou come to poverty; open thine eyes, and thou shalt be satisfied with bread." If you want God to prosper you, and you still wake up every morning with the help of an alarm clock, something is wrong. Students who would love to excel above their colleagues will not love sleep. How can a Christian sleep for 12 hours a day? Such kind of believer needs deliverance from the key of sleep.

Loving vain persons: Proverbs 28:19 says, "He that tilleth his land shall have plenty of bread: but he that followeth after vain persons shall have poverty enough." When a person is constantly found in the company of unserious people and those who don't work hard, such a person would put himself into poverty.

Laziness: Many Christians are very lazy. Instead of them to pray for ideas that would fetch them money, they would fold their hands and keep saying, "O God, we are looking at your face." Anybody who is spiritually lazy cannot get anywhere with God. If you are lazy physically, you will not get on well as well. The Christian journey is not a journey for the lazy ones.

Mocking the poor: Proverb 17: 5 says, "Whoso mocketh the poor reproacheth his Maker; and he that is glad at calamities shall not be unpunished."

People who are fond of making mockery

of the poor and laughing them to scorn shall receive the wrath of God. Don't say, "Me, I am not in your category. I am made of a better stuff. I wear only expensive clothes and not these cheap stuff that you people wear." If you have you ever looked at somebody created by God and said things like, "I don't mix up with riff raffs like you," you have mocked the poor and reproached their Maker.

You did not create them. You did not decide on your own who was going to be your parents before you were born. They too had no choice. If children had choice of parents, you would not see twins at the middle of the market with their mothers begging for bread. Mocking them is reproaching God. Sisters who tell their husbands things like, "You are a useless man. You are not like that man over there that has just bought a new fridge. You are just wasting time, you are a useless man," are mocking the poor and are reproaching his Maker who will not take it kindly with them.

Failure in tithes and offerings: Malachi 3: 8-10 says, "Will a man rob God? Yet ye have robbed me. But ye say, wherein have we robbed thee? In tithes and offerings. Ye are cursed with a curse: for ye have robbed me, even this whole nation. Bring ye all the tithes into the storehouse, that there may be meat in mine house, and prove me now herewith, saith the Lord of hosts, if I will not open you the windows of heaven, and pour you out a blessing, that there shall not be room enough to receive it." Failure in tithes and offerings is a strong key to poverty.

When you give God your tithes and offerings, don't sit down like a businessman who said, "O God, I have just paid ten thousand dollar to you and that means that you have to give me hundred thousand back. God, do you understand?" In this case, you are doing business, you are not giving. It must be willingly and cheerfully given. Believers don't borrow their tithes. If you borrow your tithe, you must pay twenty per cent on top by the time that you are bringing it back. Ten per cent is just the minimum that God wants you to bring to His house. It is different from the offerings, which you must give to God. Failure to do that would amount to God not opening you the windows of haven and pouring you out a blessing. Many believers are laboring under this curse without knowing. They always say, "I pray all the prayer

points, I did all the things that should be done
and yet nothing." The question is, are you faithful
in paying your tithe?

Not contributing to the Lord's work:
Haggai 1: 6-8 says, "You have sown much, and
bring in little; ye eat, but ye have not enough; ye
drink, but ye are not filled with drink; ye clothe
you, but there is none warm; and he that earneth
wages earneth wages to put it into a bag with
holes. Thus saith the Lord of hosts; consider
your ways. Go up to the mountain, and bring
wood, and build the house; and I will take
pleasure in it, and I will be glorified, saith the
Lord."

Anytime there is something to be done in
the church and pledges are taken, please don't be
left out even if it is only ten cent that you can
afford, Put something down for the Lord for He
sees your heart provided you have done
according to your ability. Not contributing to the
Lord's work is like watching your father's
business go down and you feel unconcerned
about it. It is this attitude that makes foolish
Christian leaders to print harvest pamphlets and
envelopes and distribute them to lodge members
because they want money.

The harvest that Jesus was talking about was the harvest of souls, not the harvest of yam and plantain and bazaar, which is really fraudulent in the house of God. It is wrong to put down a tuber of yam that someone bought for ten dollar and to start ringing bell for someone to buy it for more. Giving to God in small measures: God measures your giving by the amount you have for yourself and not by the amount you give. Jesus said that that widow contributed more than everybody did because she put all that she had. It is a pleasure when God gives you something and you are able to give it back to Him. Luke 6: 38 says, "Give, and it shall be given unto you; good measure, pressed down, and shaken together, and running over, shall men give into your bosom. For with the same measure that ye mete withal it shall be measured to you again."

Engaging in the wrong business: Luke 5: 4 – 6 says, "Now when he had left speaking, he said unto Simon, Launch out into the deep, and let down your nets for a draught. And Simon answering said unto him, Master, we have toiled all the night, and have taken nothing; nevertheless at thy word I will let down the net.

And when they had this done, they enclosed a great multitude of fishes: and their net brake..." The man who has prosperity was there, and when Peter failed, he told him what to do. When Peter saw what Jesus did, he was astonished, and those who were with him. In verse 10, Jesus said unto Simon, "Fear not; from henceforth thou shall catch men." This means that Peter was supposed to be catching men but he was busy catching fish and was not successful. Even when Jesus died, he went back to fishing and still did not catch anything- John 21: 3-6.

Not caring for ministers of God: Mathew 10: 41 says, "He that receiveth a prophet shall receive a prophet's reward; and he that receiveth a righteous man in the name of a righteous man shall receive a righteous man's reward." Ministers of God are not meant to be begging people for money. They are not supposed to be commercial ministers like it is these days. But the church of God is meant to look after its ministers.

Not giving to the poor: Proverbs 28: 27 says, "He that giveth unto the poor shall not lack: but he that hideth his eyes shall have many a curse." Giving to the poor helps you to have abundance.

The curse of poverty: Galatians 3: 13-14 says, "Christ hath redeemed us from the curse of the law, being made a curse for us; for it is written, cursed is every one that hanged on a tree…" The curse of the law includes poverty, disease and death.

Ignorance: Hosea 4: 6 says, "My people are destroyed for lack of knowledge…" Some believers are ignorant of God's provisions for their lives. Some people who claim to be living by faith tell lies because they are living by begging. Ignorance concerning the keys of prosperity or keys to success would lead to poverty. Ignorance is the major cause of human failure in many endeavors.

Pride: Some people feel that they are too big to do some jobs whereas they have no job. They would say, "This is not the kind of job for university graduates. I cannot do it." They then begin to walk about the street jobless. They always forget that God takes a little thing and then multiplies it. This is why rich illiterate men employ many university graduates today; yet they do not want to do the kind of jobs that those illiterate men did before they became rich. They feel that they are too big to begin business in a little dirty way. God will deliver all those who have the spirit of pride in them, in Jesus' name.

Ostentatious living: Some people like showing off. As soon as they collect their salary, the people they brought things from would be waiting to collect their money. They want to look better than everybody does and so they keep paying debts.

Rigidity: When a person refuses to leave a closed business, he will suffer.

Discouragement: A lot of people give up so soon. Once they fail at first attempt, they give up. Some believe that they will fail even before they start; they have programd their minds to failure. When the failure eventually comes, they will say, "I knew that it would not work." The spirit of discouragement, the spirit of the loser and the spirit of the tail are all the same thing.

Lack of good counseling: A lot of people go into things without counseling and they do not ask for God's direction. This leads to failure.

Engaging in secret sins: Sin hinders blessings. They stop God from working. As a believer, if you have some sins that you are committing secretly, you have the key of poverty in your hands.

Demonic activities: The major factors responsible for the poverty of black people in this environment are demonic activities.

God is a good Father who cares for His children and listens to them. He is always ready to hear us when we cry unto Him and satisfies our needs. He is not against us having money but does not want money to have us. You can have money as far as money does not have you, and does not get into your head. One man of God said that a man is rich by what he has left after all his money has been removed. Money can either be good or bad because a bad man's money will do bad things and a good man's money will do good things. A bad man will use his money for the kingdom of Satan while a good man will use his money for the kingdom of God.

If however you have money and you don't control it in accordance to God's will, it will control you and lead your soul to hell. Roman 12: 1 says, "I beseech you therefore, brethren, by the mercies of God, that ye present your bodies a living sacrifice, holy acceptable unto God, which is your reasonable service. And be not conformed to this world; but be ye transformed by the renewing of your mind. That ye may prove what is that good, and acceptable and perfect will of God." Your consecration to the Lord is the basic requirement for God's blessings. Have you presented yourself holy to the Lord? Sacrifices have no power over the priest. We cannot sacrifice money to the Lord and His work if we ourselves are not sacrificed. Judas thought he was doing a good thing when he threw Jesus into the hands of those who would kill Him. He did not know what he was doing but the men who wanted Jesus knew what they were doing. He collected his thirty shekels of silver without knowing that he was fulfilling an evil prophecy. He thought that Jesus would overcome His captors by His mighty power. He was surprised to see Him following them like a sheep. The money became useless and he threw it back at those who gave it to him.

Luke 16: 13 says, "No servant can serve two masters: for either he will hate the one, and love the other; or else he will hold to the one, and despise the other. Ye cannot serve God and mammon." In the foregoing, mammon is personified and treated as an idol. It is treated like another god. The Bible says that you cannot serve two masters. You cannot serve God and mammon. The word "cannot" means impossibility. You may work for two masters but you can serve only one.

Mammon

Mammon is that demon power that controls money. It is the devil's salesman. It is the power behind those who sell charms, witchcraft materials and do all kinds of things to make men sell their souls for money. Also, mammon spirit distribute spirits of poverty to attack human race particularly Christians. It is the demon that controls greediness, selfishness, poverty and financial bankruptcy. Many Christians have to defeat mammon in their lives. They have to bind the power and spirit of mammon. It is an evil spiritual power that grips men and enslaves them through money. It is the spirit that is working in the world and has made so many people to become slaves to money. We must deal this satanic force that enslaves men and women through money.

Your attitude towards money reveals your attitude towards God. If you are always ready to tell lies because of money, you cannot be a friend of God. So, your attitude towards money is very important if you want God to give you prosperity. The reason God sometimes does not give a person too much money is because He has seen some things in that person. He knows that giving such a person plenty of money would mean giving him a straight ticket to hellfire. No wonder Paul describes the love of money as the root of all evil. Whether you are poor or rich, it is either you are ruling money or money is ruling you. Poverty does not free one from the ruler ship of money. It will turn both poor and rich men to thieves. The love of money is what makes drivers of commercial vehicles to be involved in accidents most of the time. It makes people to drink terrible concoctions; it makes human beings to kill one another. Many will engage in the accumulation of money and forget their souls. Some will prefer to run their businesses on Sundays instead of coming to church. There are people who commit adultery in order to make money. The money of affliction and sin will lead to more problems.

Some people can die because of money. Some can spoil the lives of their children because of money. It is also the same reason many sisters marry the wrong men. They want good cars, expensive perfumes from Paris, expensive shirts and ties. Even when you ask them to go and pray, they will not regard it as important.

It is very bad to overestimate the power of money. Sometimes wealthy people are shocked to discover that there are things that money cannot purchase. And strangely too, poor people always imagine that once they have money, everything would be okay.

True riches are spiritual and it involves your being conformed to the image of God's Son, Jesus Christ. You need to deliver your money from the world. You need to deliver your money from your own self. If you are controlling your money or the world is controlling your money for you, it means that you have not submitted yourself to God. If you give God what you cannot feel, then you make Him a beggar. The best bank is in heaven. God cannot force you to part with your money. The money you are dying for had been in the world before you were born. When God says, give, He is just giving you a privilege, and so, don't misuse that privilege. Don't be like Solomon who spent thirteen years building his own house and seven years to build God's house. Don't be a slave to money with money. God loves a cheerful giver. What people call money carries a lot of heavy load? A dirty currency note represents both blood and toil. It is frightening because it can serve or destroy man. Only God knows the secret of how many hands the money you are holding has passed through. Only God knows the evil or the good the notes have done since the moment they were printed. The money will not speak so it will never tell you all that is hidden it. Many people would have died because of that note you are holding. Many might have killed themselves for it. Many might have fought to possess it for a few hours, or to use it for a little pleasure and joy. That money might have fed a baby; it might have provided food for a family or books for education. But at the same time, it might have sent a letter breaking an engagement. It might have been used for abortion fees. It might have bought alcohol to create a drunkard. It might have bought dirty films or might have been used to record an indecent song. It might have been used for good or bad. This is why we must always pray on our money. This is the secret behind the power of mammon to trap people.

Many Christians are holding too tight to the money that has passed through so many things instead of giving it back to God. You must understand that God does not want us to be poor. But the keys to poverty must be dropped. Understand that God gave you whatsoever you have now and you must give it back to Him. If you refuse to do that, He would look for people who will give it back to Him and bless them. Therefore, be wise.

Prayer Points

1. O God, locate and revive my divine potentials, in the name of Jesus.

2. I break every curse of poverty, in the name of Jesus.

3. You spirit of poverty, be bound, in the name of Jesus.

4. I bind the spirit drinking the blood of my blessing, in Jesus' name.

5. O Lord, create profitable opportunities for me, in the name of Jesus.

6. O God, if my job or business needs changing, change it for me, in Jesus' name.

7. O God, reveal the secret of spiritual prosperity to me, in the name of Jesus.

8. All my stolen blessings, be returned to me, in the name of Jesus.

9. I refuse to inherit the spirit of poverty, in the name of Jesus.

Chapter Two

Attack the Spirit of Jezebel

A lot of people are struggling and tiring them out with a closed door whose key they do not have. In the absence of the key, banging, shouting, crying or general struggle trying to get in, is a useless exercise. Unfortunately, this is the position of many Christians.

Jesus said unto Peter, *"I give to you the key of the Kingdom and whatever you bind on earth, shall be bound in heaven and whatever you loose on earth, shall be loosed in heaven."* Peter had a key, Paul too, had a key. I want the key that would open the door to my breakthrough physically and spiritually, in the name of Jesus.

The Lord meant our body to be His temple.

But before the glory of God can fill a particular temple, the temple has to be cleansed and purged. Therefore, Jesus had to purge the temple at Jerusalem. He said to them, "My house shall be called a house of prayer but you have turned it to a den of robbers" and He chased them out. The body of man is meant to be the temple of the Lord. But to many people, the body is not the temple of God but virtually a caged or imprisoned entity by powers greater than them. I want you to proclaim liberty and freedom to yourself. The Bible says, "If the Son makes you free, you are free indeed." It also says that where the Spirit of the Lord is, there is liberty and that Jesus came to proclaim liberty to the captive.

Please, pray like this: "Freedom from the Lord Jesus, soak me from the top of my head to the sole of my feet, in Jesus' name." The Bible says, "If God be for us, who can be against us." When God is for somebody, anyone who decides to go against that person must be mad. If a witch or wizard or powers of darkness decide to wage war against a child of God, it would be the beginning of their end. In fact, it is madness to attack a child of the most High God.

A lot of Christians never grow because they spend 90 per cent of their prayer time battling internal and external enemies and spend only 10 per cent on their spiritual growth. When the spirit of freedom is upon you, anyone who turns against you is planning to run mad. Beloved ones enough of useless battles.

In many places in the Bible, God set against themselves the enemies who prepared themselves and trained their armies to fight against the Israelites. They destroyed themselves while the Israelites moved in and collected the spoil. This is why you must pray this prayer point: "Let all the enemies of my soul get busy as from today fighting against them, in Jesus' name.

Who Is Jezebel?

The first introduction of Jezebel in the Bible portrays her as the rebellious and domineering wife of a king, called Ahab. She dominated and manipulated her husband. Unfortunately, for the nation of Israel, her husband happened to be their king. I Kings 16: 30 – 31: *"And Ahab, the son of Omri did evil in the sight of the Lord above all that was before him. And it came to pass, as if it had been a light thing for him to walk in the sins of Jeroboam the son of Nebat, which he took to wife Jezebel, the daughter of Ethbaal king of the*

Zidonians, and went and served Baal, and worshipped him." God had warned His children never to marry the Zidonians.

The warning is true today that no believer should marry an unbeliever. If you do that in spite of the fact that you know that it is wrong, you have only constructed a coffin for your home. Eventually, it will become a foundational problem that will be very difficult to solve. This was what a whole king of Israel did. Apart from that, he was serving the idol of Jezebel called Baal. My prayer for bachelors is that they will never marry Jezebels, and the spinsters too, will never marry Ahabs, in Jesus' name. Ahab raised an altar for Baal and built a house for it in Samaria.

The Bible says that Ahab did more to provoke the Lord God of Israel to anger than all the kings of Israel that were before him. His problem started when he married Jezebel.

In the book of Revelation, we see Jezebel again surfacing. Revelation 2: 20- 21 *"Notwithstanding, I have a few things against thee, because thou allow that woman Jezebel, which calleth herself a prophetess, to teach and to seduce my servants to commit fornication, and to eat things sacrificed unto idols. And I gave her space to repent of her fornication; and she repented not."*

Jezebel, the wife of Ahab, was so powerful

that she forced 10 million Jews to bow to Baal. Only about seven thousand plus Elijah were faithful to God. In fact, Elijah thought he was the only one, until God said, "No, I have seven thousand more somewhere."

The Spirit of Jezebel

The woman Jezebel is now dead physically, but the spirit of Jezebel is still very much around and has caused and is causing many problems for Christians. This spirit has thousands of people in its grip. It is responsible for the worldliness and lack of seriousness you find in Christians nowadays.

It is the spirit converting many houses of God to entertainment halls, where people just go to be entertained by actors. It is the spirit of Jezebel that has produced a lot of psychedelic and disco pastors. You see pastors with 'jerry curls' and 'Tyson' hairstyles, in such places, you cannot differentiate between the pastor's wife and a club girl. It is responsible for the conversion of the house of God to a place of merchandise and fashion parade. It is now introducing witchcraft into the house of God very cleverly and people are not aware of it. The spirit of Jezebel is responsible for the perversion of the authority in the home, where the wife is converted to the husband and the husband is converted to the wife.

Jezebel incited her husband to do evil and eventually led him into trouble with the Almighty God. God got fed up with Ahab and called a meeting of His angels and said, "Which of you will go down and deceive Ahab to die." They all gathered and gave different suggestions. All that time, Ahab was comfortable. Eventually, God put a lying spirit in the 200 prophets of Ahab. Sometimes, when one wants to go into destruction, he would be deaf to every wise counsel. All the 200 prophets prophesied and said, "Go and the Lord will give these people unto your hand." Only one man was different, a true prophet of God. He said, "No, if you go, you will not come back," and Ahab promptly commanded that he should be locked up.

The spirit of Jezebel is the spirit responsible for the revengeful spirit in many believers now. A lot of believers want to retaliate what other people did to them just like Jezebel wanted to retaliate on Elijah. This is wrong. The spirit of Jezebel is responsible for the idolatry that is in the church now. A man came to the house of God and said he was broke and that he wanted to be prayed for so that he would begin to prosper. Some brethren prayed for him, shortly after, he went to his bank account, which had been dormant for a long time and found that somebody had mistakenly paid $30,000.00 into it. He jumped up and said that the Lord had prospered him. He went ahead and withdrew the money and gave testimony that God had prospered him. That is modern idolatry.

The spirit of independence and ambition to be popular is the work of the spirit of Jezebel. It is the spirit that kills God's prophets prematurely. It is the power behind seducing spirits. The work of the spirit of Jezebel is getting so common nowadays. All the panel-beating and the spraying of the body by Christians and careless eating are the works of the spirit of Jezebel.

The Name, JEZEBEL

What does the name Jezebel mean? It means 'without co-habitation.' That is, Jezebel will not dwell with anyone,' unless she can control and dominate that person. It has destroyed preachers and politicians. It makes people to commit abortion. It is responsible for family strives and unsettled homes.

Prisoners of Jezebel

There are many secret prisoners of Jezebel today. They have no control over their sexual desire. They run after their house girls at night or any other woman, apart from their wives. Anytime they are not busy praying or clapping and singing, pictures of immorality fill their hearts. When you see a man who enjoys being in the company of girls alone, know that he has a problem. If you see a woman too, who prefers to be with men all the time, something is wrong somewhere. All these are secret prisoners of the spirit of Jezebel.

The truth is that the spirit of Jezebel would stop attacking a person only when it knows that the person can withstand it, because Jezebel's worst enemies are the prophets of God who speak against it as the true prophet of God spoke against it in the Bible. The spirit of Jezebel hates repentance, prayer, holiness, purity and has captured many modern day Christians. Some people go to church to seek deliverance, only for them to get possessed by the spirit of Jezebel. This then worsens their case.

The Four Powerful Strongmen in the Book of Revelation

The spirit of death and hell: The first strongman is the spirit of death and hell. Death is the reaper while hell is the storehouse. So, one goes to work, and the other stores what is brought back.

The spirit of the anti-Christ: This is the spirit responsible for Luke warmness. It takes people farther away from the Lord and the more somebody goes away from the Lord, the more he moves into darkness.

The spirit of Babylon: This is the spirit of compromise. Believers should not compromise their faith at all.

The spirit of Jezebel: This message is centered on this strongman.

The Age Long War

There has been an age long war going on between the spirit of Elijah and the spirit of Jezebel. Elijah represents the interest of heaven, the call to repentance and a return to God. Jezebel on the other hand, represents principalities or powers whose purpose is to hinder the work of repentance. Looking deeply into the scriptures, we can see that Elijah was very bold. But Jezebel too, was also very bold. Elijah was violent against evil while Jezebel was violent against righteousness. Elijah spoke about the ways of God while Jezebel spoke about the ways of witchcraft. This war still continues today.

In the book of I Kings that we have read, Jezebel had systematically murdered God's servants, the ones she could lay her hand upon. It was not that she did not look for Elijah, but the God of Elijah kept Elijah out of her hands. Ahab looked everywhere for Elijah and when eventually Obadiah found him, he said,

"We have searched for you everywhere. You just locked up the windows of heaven and put the key inside your pocket, the king is looking for you."

But something happened in I Kings 18. There was a contest between the prophets of Jezebel and Elijah. The contest was on Mount Carmel. The contest was very simple. The prophets of Baal, who were 450 in number, were on one side while Elijah was on the other side. Elijah said unto the people,

"I even I only, remain a prophet of the Lord; but Baal's prophets are four hundred and fifty men. Call ye on the name of your gods, and I will call on the name of the Lord; and the God that answereth by fire, let him be God. And all the people answered and said, it is well spoken."

So they began to call on the name of Baal and nothing happened. They did this for almost 12 hours. The Bible says,

"And it came to pass at the time of the offering of the evening sacrifice, that Elijah the prophet came near and said, Lord God of Abraham, Isaac and of Israel, let it be known this day that thou art God in Israel, and that I am thy servant, and that I have done all these things at thy word. Hear me, O Lord, hear me, that this people may know that thou art the Lord God, and that thou hast turned their heart back again. Then the fire of the Lord fell and consumed the burnt sacrifice, and the wood, and the stones, and the dust and licked up the water that was in the trench. And when all the people saw it, they fell on their faces; and they said, The Lord, he is the God; the Lord, He is the God. (Elijah did not stop there like many Christians would do). And Elijah said unto them, take the prophets of Baal; let no one of them escape. And they took them and Elijah brought them down to the brook Kishon, and slew them there."

And so will you slay your Baal today, in Jesus'

name.

The God of Elijah is the God of fire. He will fight for you today against any spirit of Jezebel, in the name of Jesus. Now, after this kind of super victory, why on earth should Elijah run away and say that he wanted to die. I Kings 19: 14:

"But he himself went a day's journey into the wilderness, and came and sat down under a juniper tree; and he requested for himself that he might die, and said, it is enough now, O Lord, take away my life; for I am not better than my fathers." This was Elijah talking because in verse 2, Jezebel threatened him. "Then Jezebel sent a messenger unto Elijah saying, so let the gods do unto me and more also if I make not thy life as the life of one of them by tomorrow about this time."

Fear and Discouragement

What came over the person who prayed and fire fell? How could such a mighty prophet turn and run? The answer is simple: Jezebel had released a flood of witchcraft and demonic powers against him. It was not that the witches were eating up his flesh or drinking his blood. No, they could not, but they put two things in his hearts, which are already in the heart of many people today.

The two things are fear and discouragement. When those things entered into the spirit of Elijah as a result of an attack by the spirit of Jezebel, the great prophet of fire turned and ran when he could easily have stood at the palace of Ahab and call fire down so that Jezebel and her whole household would be destroyed. He turned and ran because two of the greatest weapons of the enemy were used against him.

A lot of people think that witchcraft is only about eating their flesh, drinking their blood and breaking their legs. No.

When there is fear and discouragement in a person's spirit, the person would run even if it is only a cockroach that is talking. And then in that position of fear, the person becomes an easy target for the enemy. They would be able to touch the person because he has not placed sufficient fire around himself. Witchcraft would first of all send its two disciples; fear and discouragement. If you allow them to touch you, then they start clearing the road. They discourage people so much that they would not be able to pray well and you would be thinking it is one man somewhere. These two powerful weapons are what the spirit of Jezebel uses a lot today.

Elijah went away in his chariot of fire. John the Baptist came in the spirit and power of Elijah. And the dancing daughter of Herodias got John killed. She danced very well and Herod the king promised to give whatever she wanted. The girl now said, "I want the head of John the Baptist." So, the man who came with the spirit and power of Elijah was killed just like that.

What the spirit of Jezebel did to Elijah, Herodias, too, did it to John the Baptist. But before John was beheaded, the two evil disciples of Jezebel had attacked him; that is fear and discouragement. It was so much that John sent a messenger to Jesus asking, "Are you the one that is to come or should we look for another?" Here was the forerunner of Jesus Christ who said, "Behold the Lamb of God, who taketh away the sins of the world." He baptized Jesus yet, he sent a messenger to Him to find out because fear and discouragement had entered into him.

The Spirit of Elijah

The ministry of Elijah is not over. In fact, the book of Malachi tells us that towards the end of time, God will still send Elijah to us. Malachi 4: 5 –

6: "Behold, I will send you Elijah the prophet before the coming of the great and dreadful day of the Lord. And he shall turn the heart of the fathers to the children, and the heart of the children to their fathers lest I come and smite the earth with a curse."

God is still raising up a company of Prophet Elijah. These are Spirit -filled Christians who are supposed to kill the prophets of Jezebel and to drink the blood of the prophets of Baal. But you cannot be in the company of Elijah if Jezebel still has a hold on you. If your enemy cannot attack you directly, he would seek to bring you into sin, thereby positioning you for the judgment of God. That is true about the enemy.

The movement of the power of the spirit of Elijah is what we need now to put the spirit of Jezebel to flight. Addiction, adultery, arrogance, broken marriages, fear, fornication, jealousy, unclean thoughts, masturbation, perverted sexual relationships, spiritual blindness, the spirit of religion, witchcraft and all occult involvement manifest in the lives of those who are controlled by the spirit of Jezebel. For example, if the spirit of Esau were upon somebody, the person would sell his birthright, meaning that the person would stay at the tail instead of at the head.

If the spirit of Menasseh were upon somebody, the person would also operate at the tail region. If the spirit of Pisgah were upon somebody, the person would be seeing good things but would never taste them. If the spirit of Saul were upon somebody, the person would start off on fire for God and end up with the spirit of witchcraft. If the spirit of Pharaoh or Herod were upon somebody, good things would die at infancy in their lives.

The spirit of Jezebel is the spirit that kills God's anointing in people's life. Such people would receive no revelation. They pray and see nothing or hear nothing. This spirit kills the prophet inside of you. It is the spirit that pushes people under God's judgment like it happened to Ahab. Jezebel kept pushing Ahab until he entered into trouble. The spirit of Jezebel is the spirit that prefers artificial glory to the glory of God. It is the spirit that causes constant strife in the home. It turns husbands into babies and wives into giants. It is the spirit of immoral activities.

2 Kings 9: 30 −33: "And when Jehu was come to Jezebel, Jezebel heard of it; and she painted her face, and tired her head, and looked out at a window. And as Jehu entered in at the gate, she said, Had Zimri peace, who slew his master? And he lifted up

his face to the window, and said,

Who is on my side? Who? And there looked out to him two or three eunuchs. And he said, Throw her down. So they threw her down: and some of her blood was sprinkled on the wall, and on the horses; and he trod her under foot."

Beloved, today, you have to throw the spirit of Jezebel out of your life. Let the dogs lick her blood and you will trample upon it. Jehu had no mercy for Jezebel. He was not ready to reform Jezebel. There should be no mercy or compromise or sympathy towards the spirit of Jezebel. Jehu trampled her under foot. Right now, God is giving you the spirit to participate in the internal judgment of Jezebel. You have to cast her down, let the judgment of God come forth. It is time for the children of God to unite against this spirit with the power of the Holy Spirit, under the Elijah anointing and the anger of Jehu. Start to proclaim holy war against the spirit of Jezebel.

WAY OUT

There are six ways to deal with the spirit of Jezebel operating in the home. The devil tries to keep people from understanding these facts.

Do not raise your voice against your spouse because the Bible says that a soft answer turneth away wrath.

Identify the issue.

Do not dig up old wounds. Bringing up old wounds will bring up further tension.

Do not call your spouse names. This is character assassination.

Do not generalize by telling your spouse, "You always do this or do that." All these are destructive exaggeration.

Finish the discussion. Do not burst into tears or get out of the house in anger.

PRAYER POINTS

1. Please pray the following prayer points with holy anger.
2. You spirit of Jezebel, I command you to release your captives, in Jesus' name.
3. You spirit of Jezebel, you will not kill the prophet of God inside of me, in Jesus' name.
4. I cast down every evil imagination against me, in the name of Jesus.
5. I break any ungodly association with the spirit world, in the name of Jesus.
   a. Lord, set my enemies in array against themselves, in the name of Jesus.

6. The key to open the way unto my breakthrough physically and spiritually, Lord give it to me, in the name of Jesus.
7. I pull down the altar of witchcraft against my life, in the name of Jesus.

Chapter Three

Holy Troublemakers

2 Samuel 22:35-43:"He teacheth my hands to war so that a bow of steel is broken by mine arms. Thou hast also given me the shield of thy salvation, and thy gentleness hath made me great. Thou hast enlarged my steps under me, so that my feet did not slip. I have pursued mine enemies and destroyed them, and turned not again until I had consumed them. And I have consumed them, and wounded them that they could not arise, yea they are fallen under my feet.

For thou hast girded me with strength to

battle, them that rose up against me hast thou subdued under me. Thou hast also given me the necks of mine enemies, that I might destroy them that hate me. They looked, but there was none to save. Even unto the Lord, but he answered them not. Then did I beat them as small as the dust of the earth. I did stamp them as the mire of the street, and did spread them abroad."

We need more troublemakers in the church today. God is looking for holy troublemakers, that is, men and women who are filled with the Holy Ghost and would stir up trouble for the enemy. Why? Because Satan is waging war against God's people. God has called us to be soldiers. He has not called us to be parasites, benchwarmers or politicians.

God has called us to be aggressive soldiers. So, He is looking for holy troublemakers, spiritually aggressive people. This year, we must get spiritually aggressive. The Bible says that our weapons of warfare are not carnal, not political, but spiritual. We alone can make the difference and the power to determine whether things go on positively or negatively rests on the church.

It is true that some people have programd certain things into the sun, moon and the stars and thereby limiting others. It is only the church of God that can pull down these altars that are mounted above. We need to be spiritually aggressive in order to be able to do that. We need an army of troublemakers now who will stir up and challenge all the established dead churches, satanic strongholds, wicked institutions, witchcraft covens, and all the evil arrangements in the heavenliness.

There are some people who can take a person's name and program it into the moon and the stars because they don't want the person to rise. And the person would never make progress and will be ruined if nothing is done urgently. So, it is not the kind of thing you smile at. It is something to be spiritually aggressive about. The Lord is looking for holy troublemakers who will challenge this kind of thing.

Sometime ago, a group of evangelists went out to preach in a place where there were a lot of satanic strongholds. They went to the first man and said, "We have come to talk to you about Jesus." He said, "Jesus? I am coming." By the time he came back, the first person dropped his Bible and slept off, and before you know it, all the ten of them fell down and slept off. He then woke them up and said, "Don't come here again," and drove them away. They quickly picked up their Bibles and ran away, totally embarrassed. Now, those were people who were supposed to be Holy Ghost filled.

We see the testimony of the apostles in Acts. 15:26 which says, "Men that have hazarded their lives for the name of our Lord Jesus Christ." They considered their lives to be nothing. They committed their lives to God and God was with them. God worked with them. Anywhere they went, signs and wonders followed them. People knew that they came there. If we are ever going to move our environment for God, we must follow their examples. In Acts 16:20, we see another testimony of those who started what we are doing now. It says, "And brought them to the magistrates, saying, these men, being Jews, do exceedingly trouble our city." Also, Acts. 17: 6 says, "And when they found them not, they drew Jason and certain brethren unto the rulers of the city crying, these that have turned the world upside down are come hither also."

So the kingdom of Christ has come to turn things around. Paul and Silas were two of the greatest troublemakers we see in the Bible. They were going through a city and one girl was crying after them saying,

"These men are the servants of the highest God, who have come to preach the way of salvation."

The girl was saying the right thing but with the wrong spirit. Paul, the holy troublemaker, allowed the girl to cry for three days and after that he turned against the spirit inside her and rebuked it, saying, "Get out of her, you foul spirit," and the serpentine spirit left her. When Paul cast out the demon in her and there was uproar in the whole city. The people who were making money with her, caused trouble. Eventually, the apostles were beaten, dragged on the floor and put into the innermost part of the jail and chained. What these men did was to turn the city upside down. When they got to the prison, they started singing and commotion happened the following day.

They caused an earthquake and the prison doors got broken and their chains fell off. But with all these they did not run out of the prison. When the guards wanted to kill themselves, they told them not to do so, that they would not escape. To add to this, they demanded an apology and those they be escorted out of the prison. Eventually, the authorities apologized to them and asked them to go.

God is looking for such people now. That is, men and women who understand what the Bible means by, "They overcame him by the blood of the Lamb and by the words of their testimonies. And they loved not their lives unto death," meaning that they have donated their lives to Jesus. The Bible says that whosoever wants to save his life shall lose it.

Sometime ago, a pastor friend of mine was invited to a street which was full of herbalists. Each of their signboards was larger than that of the church. People trooped to them day and night. This annoyed the spirit of the pastor, unlike some Christians who would see this kind of thing but it would not annoy their spirit. So, every day, at 2 a.m. the pastor went to these buildings, pointed at them one after the other and prayed like this: "You powers of darkness that are helping herbalists to operate here, evaporate from here and condense into hell fire, in Jesus' name."

After he did this for a month, the herbalists called a meeting to decide what to do. They could not face the pastor and they waited for the day his General Overseer came. They went to the General Overseer and said, "Sir, that your dog you put here, restrain him or bring the former pastor back." The former pastor was not disturbing them. When the General Overseer heard that, he could not believe his ears. He was amazed at the way these people with the powers of darkness spoke openly.

The truth is that God would manifest His power only to those who stand up against the forces of hell, and not to those who are still busy struggling with simple things. God would manifest His power only to those who stand against the forces of darkness and not to those who are still fighting their wives and husbands at home instead of fighting the devil. The devil may rage, the powers that be may threaten, but God has all the power, and will stand by you when you take a stand. The secret of Shadrach, Meshach and Abednego was that they took a stand against the devil.

The Almighty was happy with them and He came to their aid. But when you compromise, and you are neither here nor there, God, too, cannot stand by you. All the singing and praying that do not touch people's lives must stop. The counselors must counsel with fire. The prayer teams must take their proper positions, not the type of praying teams that would be meeting and witches are busy with their own discussions there. All the evangelism without fire must stop. The city and the country must know that Jesus is Lord.

We need more sisters who will be aggressive for Jesus; we need more brothers who will know the

Bible more than they know the names of perfumes. We need more actions. We need to spit more fire.

A certain pastor came to me complaining that his church was not growing. He complained that so and so were disturbing him. I simply told him that his problem was because he had no fire in his life. I encouraged him to seek the fire of God and watch what would happen. He went back to his station, did as I told him and things began to happen. In that city which was under the stronghold of the children of the bondwoman, was a popular mad woman. Everybody knew her because she had a small dustbin in every corner of the town. One day, while the pastor and his men were clearing the ground they found her, they laid hands on her and prayed for her. Suddenly, she said, "Why am I wearing this? What am I doing here? Where are my children?"

Then it was clear that she had been healed. That miracle alone brought a lot of people to the church. Before then, the pastor was busy apportioning blame. But when the fire came, he became a holy troublemaker. We must get hold of the horns of the altar and refused to let them go.

What do I mean by that? It means that we should pursue the enemy by aggressive prayer and by appropriating the blood of Jesus. The Bible teaches that we must pursue our enemies and overcome them. Through the power of the Holy Spirit we can be victorious over the enemies. The enemies should be running away from us not us running away from them. For example, if you have a person who is possessed in your place of work, he should be the one avoiding you and not you avoiding him. David pursued his enemies until they were destroyed and consumed. He did not rest until his enemies were destroyed. A lot of us have become comfortable cohabiting with the enemy. But if you are wearing your full spiritual armor, the enemy should be running away from you.

Sometime ago, a madman was brought to one of our meetings. He was very violent. So, the prayer warriors prayed that the Lord should put him to sleep and he slept off. His people carried him home still sleeping. He slept for two days before he woke up.

The woman with whom he was sharing a shop in the market came to the house and asked of him and was told that he was in. She did not believe it until she was led to his room where she met him sitting up, lusty and hearty. She said, "What did you do to him to make him normal?" They said, "Prayers in the name of Jesus." She went home, slept and when she woke up, she ran mad. There had been a reverse. That is what we call 'back to sender.'

So, our prayers must be backed up with fire, and likewise our Bible reading and all our other actions. Our prayers must be backed up with our actions. Elijah was a powerful man of prayer. There is no Bible student who will dispute that. But after he had prayed, he backed up his prayers with actions. He challenged the prophets of Baal to a contest. Elijah was not the only prophet around that time. There were others who were hid in the caves and were fed with bread and water. They were silent, unknown and afraid. But Elijah, the troublemaker, came out, and even the king called him a troublemaker. He told the king that he and his father's house were the troublers of Israel.

Elijah killed 450 prophets of Baal. I pray that you will kill your prophet of Baal today, in Jesus' name. Elijah was not a gentleman to the devil. He openly mocked the prophets of Baal. He knew that Baal had powers but just as he had locked up heaven and put the keys in his pocket, he locked up the powers of Baal. He knew that they were not going to come there. So he mocked and ridiculed them. Gentlemen don't do things like that.

The Bible says that the righteous shall be as

bold as the lion. Jesus Himself was a troublemaker. He drove people away from the temple and called the religious leaders of His time serpents, the blind, white sepulchers and brood of vipers. He even said to some people, "You are of your father, the devil." Those were not the words of a gentleman.

Unfortunately, many churches today are filled with silent, delicate and fragile gentlemen and women, spiritual diplomats who do not want any trouble. They would say, "I like the way I am doing my own things quietly, I don't want to be too fanatical. If I go beyond this, my family members will call a meeting and ask me to take it easy with this my new religion." That is why the kingdom of the Lord is called an upside down kingdom. The values of the world are not ours. What the world cherishes is dung to us. We do not run after the same things as the world because we know that our citizenship is not here. We are going to a better country, a city without foundation. So, there are certain things that we do not bother ourselves about.

Some people would say, "Stop preaching to me. Don't pray for me anymore. Don't force your religion on me" They would scream and scream, but such things do not bother holy troublemakers. They still continue. I read a story about a man called

Charles Finney.

One day, as he was taking a stroll, he found a man leaning on a pole, smoking hemp. He went to the man and said, "Jesus loves you. Why are you smoking this?" The man got angry and told him that what he was doing with his life was none of his business. Mr. Finney smiled and said, "With due respect, sir, what you are doing concerns me. As an evangelist, it is my business." The fellow asked him to get away. He went away. But three nights later, somebody came banging on his door. When he opened the door, he found the same man he had preached the gospel to crying. The man said, "Since the night you spoke to me I have had no peace. I want to give my life to Jesus." That was how the man got born again.

The Ministry Of Philip

This is a year that every serious Christian should receive Philip's kind of ministry. What is Phillip's kind of ministry? Act 8: 5-8 s; "Then Phillip went down to the city of Samaria, and preached Christ unto them and the people with one accord gave heed unto those things which Philip spoke, hearing and seeing the miracles which he did. For unclean spirits crying with loud voice, came out of many that were possessed with them, and many taken with palsies, and that were lame, were healed. And there was great joy in that city." Philip was not an ordained pastor. He was just a layman filled with the Holy Ghost. He was not a pulpit man but a layperson who believed in the power of the Holy Ghost. Philip went everywhere expecting miracles to happen. He was the man of the marketplace but he caused things to happen. We need to imbibe his kind of ministry.

For Christians to make an impact on the nation or city where they are, they must become Christ-consumed and Holy Spirit-filled like Philip. We must become evangelists with faith to cast out evil spirits and pray for salvation and healing of others. Don't stay where you were last year. Some people before they were blessed with cars, came to services early. Now that they have cars they come late and give all kinds of excuses. If they do not say that the carburetor of their car is faulty, they would say that their drivers came late. So, they are blaming God for the breakthrough. Where do we go from here?

A certain minister was sent to a town in the West African coast region. When he got there, he decided to visit the chief priest whom he learnt was the one causing trouble in the place. The chief priest said, "My dear pastor, I will demonstrate something to you now." He picked a piece of maize and placed it on his palm and instantly the maize started to grow on his palm. The pastor watched him and was very scared. The chief then asked him if his God could do that. He did not have an answer, and he quickly looked for an excuse and ran back to Nigeria. Later, another minister was posted there. He also went to the chief priest, who began to demonstrate his demonic power again. He put the maize in his palm and it started to grow as usual. The brother watched, and the priest said, "Can your God do this?" The brother said, "No. My God does not waste time on things like this but I will show you a little bit of what my God can do. He then opened his mouth and said, "You satanic maize, be roasted, in the name of Jesus." And the chief priest cried out, "My hand, my hand." After the maize had roasted, the fire began to burn his hand." The brother had to pray for his hand to heal. That was a troublemaker.

Where do we go from here? Do we want to continue our Christian race with such complaints as 'something is pressing me down on my bed', 'something is pursuing me.' or 'I saw a snake.' 'I saw water and I wanted to cross and one woman said I should not cross?' Would we allow the children of the bondwoman and the children of darkness to sit on our wealth and we will be watching them and believe that well, one day, something will happen? No. Nothing will happen until we begin to pray and address what should be addressed. Then things will start changing. The spirit of demonic silence must go. Many of us are too quiet about the things of God.

If you are a boss somewhere, buy tracts, put them on your table and distribute to those who come to see you. Don't sit in the bus and sleep. If you open your mouth wide and preach, there is no way you will fall asleep. God will only commit Himself to those who will take a stand.

Create time for evangelism. The reason God puts you where you are for you to reach out to some people. And if you are a failure there, it will be a disaster for the Almighty. You never know what you can do until you try.

Sometime ago, the daughter of a certain sister had a mental problem and she was very wild. She took her to the hospital where she was given a special room because the drugs were not working. She bounced on anybody who tried to enter into the room. One day, the sister listened to a message entitled, "You, the sleeping giant, stir up yourself." After listening to the message, she went to the hospital and asked to see her daughter. They told her to talk to her from the window. She said no, that she would like to enter the room. She entered and when the daughter saw her, she became wild. But the sister said, "In the name of Jesus, you wild beast, come out of her now." It was as if she gave a punch to the girl. She fell down and straightaway she said, "Mummy." She became calm as she was delivered from the evil spirit troubling her.

The sister was shocked that she could do it. God will not commit Himself to those who would just sit down at home, or to men who after Sunday service, would sit down at home and watch television, who are not interested in house fellowship or group activities.

PRAYER POINTS
1. Anything programed into the moon and the star against me, I dismantle you, in Jesus' name.
2. Lay your hands on your head and say: Power, prosperity and purity, fall upon me now, in Jesus' name.

3. Any evil thing programed into this week against me, I dismantle you, in Jesus' name.
4. Lord, I need your strength; I want to move out for you, in Jesus' name.
5. Any sickness programed into my life, fall down and die, in the name of Jesus.
6. Every evil thing programed into my life, fall down and die, in the name of Jesus.
7. I disconnect my life from every spirit of failure, in Jesus' name.
8. My life, refuse to invite failure, in the name of Jesus.
9. Holy Spirit, overshadow my life, in Jesus' name.
10. The enemy that does not want to let me go, be buried alive, in the name of Jesus.
11. Every evil bird monitoring my life, I pluck out your eyes, in Jesus' name.

Chapter Four

I Need a Miracle

2 Chronicles 16:9: "For the eyes of the Lord run to and fro throughout the whole earth, to show him strong in the behalf of them whose heart is perfect toward him..."

Every day, God watches out for an opportunity to do a great thing for you when your heart is perfect towards him. Anyone who claims that he does not need a miracle must be somebody without goals in life. We are all in need of miracles and thank God, we have the God of miracles.

What Is A Miracle?

It is an event beyond the power of any human

being; an event beyond any physical law. it is a supernatural occurrence or a wonderful thing brought about by the power of God. Sometimes the Bible refers to it as mighty works or marvelous things. When God does it, He does it to His own glory. Anywhere you see human beings, miracles are needed. Paul the apostle had been inside a ship for a long time and the people with him in the ship refused to listen to the voice of God. Rather, they listened to the devil and started to reap the result. Sailing became dangerous and they spent a long time on the sea in anguish. Most of them stopped eating. They threw their luggage into the sea and it was dark for many days. They had given up hope on living. To worsen the situation, the ship in which they were traveling, hit a rock and was shattered to pieces. But one way or the other, they all got to the shore on splinters of wood. When they got to the shore, Apostle Paul, the man of God sat down to warm himself by the fire and a viper jumped out of the woods and fastened to his hand, wanting to disgrace him. All other prisoners and the sailors were there. It did not go for them. I do not know which serpent has fastened itself to your own hand but one thing I know is that God can shake it into the fire. That was what happened to Paul. As the people there were waiting for him to fall down and die, thinking he was evil, he shook the snake into the fire and did not fall down neither did he die. When they found that he did not die, they changed their mind and gathered around him as he continued to demonstrate the power of God in their midst. So the disgrace that the enemy planned for him was converted into a revival. God is still in that businesses of having His children throw serpents into the fire. Paul threw the snake away and its poison had no effect on him. That was a miracle.

If miracles work contrary to human logic then you expect the unusual or the unexpected to happen whenever you are praying for a miracle. If you were going to be looking at what your biology or sciences say, you would be far from miracles. When you come to God, know that what you considered to be logical would be illogical to Him. What you think is completely illogical may be the right thing to God. The Bible makes us to understand that God still works miracles.

Unfortunately, these days, many people do not agree that the human brain has its own limit. Anything such people cannot understand with their brain, they just conclude it cannot happen. What a shallow way of looking at things.

Once the brain perceives certain things as impossible, the human mind accepts it quickly and sometimes, when we accept it like that, our faith would not go beyond what we have accepted. Then, we end up insulting God. It is an insult to limit God. God often looks at us when we limit Him and He would be saying: "This people cannot realize that I created these things and I can readjust and rearranged them." When God is in operation, He specializes on things that people say is impossible. Those who are close to God, obedient to Him, and have faith in Him will always experience His miracle working power. This is why we need to cry unto Him saying: "Lord, I need a miracle." If you cry unto Him like that and He sees your heart, He will respond.

God works His miracle for several reasons and He does not have to consult anybody before doing it. He may do it just to teach a lesson, to enable men to declare the gospel properly, to silence false prophets, to reveal the devil as a destroyer, or to reveal His goodness or to reveal Jesus, the resurrection and life.

Who Needs A Miracle?

Perhaps familiar faces are troubling you in your dreams, you need a miracle. Perhaps you notice that your life has been converted to a material for testing new satanic weapons, you need a miracle. Perhaps you have been sitting for satanic examinations in your dream, which has turned you to a student in the school of tribulation, you need a miracle. Perhaps your spiritual life is stagnant, you have been struggling on your own and trying your best, but you find that you are not making progress, perhaps there are hidden and clever devourers working against you, just sucking your money and resources away, you need a miracle.

Perhaps you have what we call weak breakthroughs. By the time you have a breakthrough, there would be sufficient debts on ground to swallow it. Although there is a breakthrough but the breakthrough is not sufficient to carry the load that you have. You need a miracle. Perhaps you notice that your life is following an evil family pattern; everybody in your family is heading towards one wrong direction, for example, you notice that in your family, nobody has a good job, nobody has good health, people die young or people are not getting married, you need a miracle.

Perhaps you know that your names are placed on evil altars somewhere and someone you don't even know chants incantations on them, you need a miracle to destroy the satanic priest at the altar and to set the altar on fire. Perhaps you have been suffering from prayer paralysis. You find that you can only pray for a short time or else you develop migraine or become afraid, it would seem as if some forces want to overshadow you, you need a miracle. There are many people who have benefits abroad which foreign demons have captured. Such people need a miracle to release those things. There are many people who have been duped even by white men, they need a miracle. There are many people as well who have been cursed by satanic prophets for no just cause, some have the mark of hatred on them, those who liked them suddenly began to hate them passionately, some are suffering from leaking pockets, money comes in and goes out, they cannot retain it, they need a miracle.

I was talking to one man about the gospel and he was saying all kinds of blasphemy against the Lord Jesus Christ. I said, "O Lord, give me a word for this man, that he would know that you are the Lord." And the Lord said, "Ask him whether or not he sees himself roaming about in the market place anytime he gets his salary and he would feel as something is passing down through his pocket." I threw the question directly at him as the Lord had said it. He was surprised and asked: "Who told you that?" I said, "The same Jesus that you called a bastard now." Anyone whose pocket leaks in the spirit cannot retain money physically. He would not be able to give account of how he spends his money. Perhaps you have medical problems that defy medicine, you need a miracle. Perhaps all roads to progress seem blocked. Anywhere you go, it would seem as if someone had already gotten there before you and put a stumbling block on your way, you need a miracle. Perhaps you notice that any time you have a particular dream, a particular problem would start, you need a miracle. Perhaps you have no good job or business, you need a miracle.

Perhaps your family is under attack and they are being bombarded everyday by the arrows of the enemy or you have a building you cannot finish because witches have urinated on it, you need a miracle to remove your building from their grip. Perhaps you have answered to demonic calls; you need a miracle to cancel the evil call. Perhaps you are being tormented by very intelligent wicked network and you don't really know who your friends are or who your enemies are, you need a miracle. Perhaps you never really enjoy divine benefits. You just hear God blesses people but the only blessing you receive is that you are alive and breathing, you need a miracle. Perhaps you have open, unrepentant and stubborn household wickedness, you need a miracle. Perhaps you are suffering from intensive marital attacks, you need a miracle. A sister whose husband had abandoned for a long time, was ministered to in Kaduna. After the ministration, she took some prayer points home and prayed. After the prayers, her husband came back. He could no longer recognize his own children because they were very young when he ran away. But the sister started to complain that she did not know if it was even right for the man to come back again because the same Ankara dress that he was wearing when he left was still the same one he was wearing when he came back after many years. His lot had not improved. Perhaps your case is like that, you need a miracle. Perhaps you are one of the so many people who are born again but cannot even locate the enemy. They just know that there are enemies but cannot locate them and cannot fire their bullets properly, you need a miracle. Perhaps you are a student but you always fail your examinations, or the enemy has converted you into a foot mat; all the inferior people are promoted above you but you taught them the job, you need a miracle.

Perhaps life has become like a prison and you wish to die, you need a miracle. Perhaps you are suffering from intensive financial embarrassment, you need a miracle. When some people in this fellowship started coming here, people used to give them transport money to come and to go but now such people give tithes of $50,000. What happened to them? They received their miracle.

Perhaps you find that you are spiritually cold, or all those who want to assist you suddenly become unwilling to help, you need a miracle. Perhaps you have good ideas but there is no capital for you to work with, you need the God that turned the fish into a bank. Perhaps as one problem is going another one is coming or you are the kind of person who always fights and struggles before you can get anything done, you need a miracle.

Perhaps you have children that have traveled abroad and are doing well, but they have completely forgotten you here. And you are wallowing in poverty. Perhaps you are occupying the wrong position in your dream, you see yourself in three-piece suit, dressing well, inside a very fine car but in the physical you cannot afford a bicycle. You need a miracle. Perhaps your promotion is being denied or delayed. You need a miracle. Perhaps your marriage is the type they can call the cat and mouse marriages. You need a miracle.

Perhaps the enemy has converted your business to a desert, you need a miracle. I cannot understand how a person would take food down to the market place for sale and bring it back home without selling one grain. Such a person needs a miracle. The devil has turned the lives of so many Christians upside down so much that what is supposed to be normal, they see it as unusual. Perhaps your account is dead, you need a miracle. Don't limit God. He does not use your arithmetic to operate. He operates in a way that is beyond your imagination.

Perhaps you have accumulated debts and you don't know where to run, or your situation is so bad that you have closed your door to visitors and have given your children strict instruction that the only person they can open the door for is your pastor, you need a miracle. Perhaps you notice that your virtue has been transferred, you are supposed to be the first born but your younger ones are doing better than you, you need a miracle.

Perhaps you know you are being bewitched. When you get money your hands and body would be shaking and you put it in the wrong place, do the wrong business, and buy the wrong things, you need a miracle. Perhaps you have a dead organ in your body, you need a miracle. Perhaps you are being pursued by the spirit of death or the arrow of poverty, you need a miracle. Perhaps you are a spiritual spectator; you are just observing everything. When they say, "Receive ye the Holy Ghost," your spirit is as cold as ice block. Your own child is prophesying but you as daddy or mummy cannot see beyond your nose, you need a miracle.

Perhaps you have been feeding your enemies to fight you harder, you need a miracle. Perhaps you have long standing infirmity or you have a vagabond anointing. You cannot settle down on something, you are fishing in the ocean of life but catching nothing, you need a miracle.

Perhaps you have what we call verbal trap. The devil has recorded many messages from your mouth, and have used it to cage you because you are the one saying them, you need a miracle. Perhaps your business is suffering from what we call profit starvation, you need a miracle.

GOD'S MIRACLE AGENT

Genesis 1: 1–3: "In the beginning, God created the heaven and the earth. And the earth was without form, and void; and darkness was upon the face of the deep. And the Spirit of God moves upon the face of the waters. And God said, Let there be light: and there was light."

The Spirit of God moved upon the face of the waters. It was after that that God spoke and things began to happen. In the Bible, we can see that God did a lot of miracles through Moses. Moses was so close to God that the anointing upon him was so tremendous. At a stage, God took part of the Spirit that was upon him and divided it amongst seventy people. What was the secret of the miracle working power upon Moses? It was the anointing of the Holy Spirit. The Holy Spirit is God's miracle agent. Do you know the secret of Joseph's success in Egypt? Why was he so much in tune with God? It was because the Spirit of God was in him. Bezaleel the son of Uri was the first spiritual artist in the Bible. He constructed the furniture in the tabernacle. How did he do it? He did it by the Holy Spirit.

David was a successful king and warrior because he had the Holy Spirit. He said, "Take not thy Holy Spirit away from me." Elijah operated in the miraculous and worked wonders for the Lord. The Bible talks about the spirit and the power of Elijah. Elisha received the double portion of that spirit because he recognized that no miracle would happen without the Spirit of God. He waited for the anointing and it came upon him and that wonderful passage in

Isaiah 10:27: "...And the yoke shall be destroyed because of the anointing." The miraculous birth of Jesus was done through the power of the Holy Spirit. The angels told Mary that the Spirit of the Most high God shall overshadow her.

Luke 5:17: "And it came to pass on a certain day, as he was teaching, that there were Pharisees and doctors of the law sitting by, which were come out of every town of Galilee; and Judea, and Jerusalem, and the power of the Lord was present to heal them."

The power of God has to be present for healing to take place. A lot of people don't like the Mountain of Fire and Miracles Ministries because it is 'a do it yourself' ministry. This place demystifies priesthood and removes the veil of pastors. We make people to understand that they too can walk in the supernatural. It is not for pastors alone.

A certain white man received a touch of fire and one day, his wife woke up and found him praying on their cooker, that the cooker should work, in Jesus' name. She tapped him and said, "John, what kind of madness is this? If the cooker is not working any longer, buy another one." He said, "No. I cannot waste my money. It must work." And behold, it started working. Meaning that the miraculous can work with animate and inanimate things.

The power of the Holy Spirit is God's miracle working power. The Bible says that God anointed Jesus with the Holy Spirit and power and He went about doing good, healing those that were oppressed, for God was with Him. Jesus moved under the anointing.

The apostles too moved by the power of the Holy Spirit, any meeting where the Holy Spirit does not come down and flow freely, there will be no miracle. The Holy Spirit will not come down or move freely if He is grieved or quenched. Once you rebel against Him, He will move away quietly and nothing happens. The Holy Spirit can be resisted. What does it mean to resist the Holy Spirit? It means to rebel against His conviction.

When people refuse to surrender all to Jesus,

they experience only small miracles and those who do not believe that nothing much can happen would only expect minor miracles. Once you come to God with the expectation that He has all the powers and can do all things, you will receive miracles. But when you come to the house of God, and before the prayers start, your spirit is already low and down, the Holy Spirit will pass you by. The same thing applies to those who come to service and do not concentrate.

Miracles will not happen in such lives. Some people come to the church meditating on their problems. During prayers, such people just shake their heads and say nothing and so nothing happens. God wants us to come to Him with high expectation. You do not come to a meeting and say, "Well I am going again, I hope God will hear me today." You don't come to God like that. You should come to God with high expectation.

The Greatest Miracle

We must know that the greatest miracle we can have is our salvation. When that is taken care of, other things would follow. So if you are not saved better get saved now. We thank God for His mercies. Salvation is offered free of charge. Some people say, "I just want a miracle, I don't want to be born again." We must know that a person may get a miracle and still go to hell fire, all those who say, "I don't want to be saved. I don't want those restrictions. They don't allow you to have a mind of your own." If that is your own opinion about it, I counsel you to change your mind. And if you say you won't change your mind or surrender completely to Jesus, a time will come when you will leave this earth and you will knock at His gate and He too will look at you and say, "Who is that rebel, clear out of that place."

Even if you stand and begin to say, "But I was born in Italian Catholic church and my father was the chief usher of the Kerosene and paraffin church and my Mother was the most senior mother in Israel in our church or I was born in Elijah Apostolic church and was brought up in supernatural Anglican and now you say I should not enter," He will not open for you.

A lot of people fail examinations because they did not prepare very well. You only get what you are ready and prepared to receive. The sower went out to sow. Nothing was wrong with the sower and nothing was wrong with the seed. It was the soil that had some problems.

You have to make yourself available to God. Drop worry and anxiety and make yourself available to Him. Doctors do not go about the streets asking people if they are sick. Clothes sellers do not go about the street saying to people, "You are wearing rags, buy new clothes." Likewise barbers do not drag people from the street into their shops, saying, "Your hair is bushy, come and cut it." Soap sellers do not force people to buy soap even if they smell. Be prepared. Before Jacob's name could be changed, he got alone with God. He became spiritually aggressive in prayer.

There was a preparation. Before the wall of Jericho fell down, the Israelites marched round it for seven days. There was a preparation. Before the widow of Zarephath could receive abundance, she gave up everything she had to the prophet. In spite of the fact that she knew there was nothing else to fall back on, before Naaman could be healed, he dropped his pride, obeyed the prophet and took a bathe in the dirty water. There was a preparation.

Before that woman could receive abundance of oil, the man of God told her to go and get more vessels. God began to fill the vessels and the miracle continued for as long as there were vessels to be filled.

Identify what you need now. There is no point for a person to come before the living God, the limitless God with unbelief in his heart or without the faith that a lot of things could happen. You ought to offer a holy cry to the Lord that: "Lord, I need a miracle!"

Before we go into the prayer session, I counsel you to give your life to Christ in case you are not yet born again because I want you to experience the miracle power of God and the deliverance power of the Almighty. I want you to see the impossible happen. If you are ready to do so, make the following confession: "Lord Jesus, I am a sinner. I want to get born again. Come into my life. Forgive me my sins and cleanse me with your blood. I say bye to the devil. I enter into the kingdom of heaven, thank you Jesus, in Jesus' name. Amen."

We have to take steps to arrest every evil progress. No evil progress must continue. It is important we take this step. Perhaps you have been suffering for a long time, it is time to deliver yourself from the bondage of the enemy. The first thing to do is to break the stumbling blocks and clear the blockages away before we begin to cry to the Lord for a miracle.

Remember blind Bartimeaus threw away his garment that was disturbing him so that he might reach the Savior. We must also fling away every evil garment now so that we can touch the Savior. Raise your voice like thunder as you take the following prayer points:

PRAYER POINTS
1. I receive spiritual violence to confuse my enemies, in the name of Jesus.
2. Every satanic angel blocking my breakthroughs is bound, in the name of Jesus.
3. God that answereth by fire, answer my prayer now by fire, in the name of Jesus.
4. Every power making my miracle to slip out of my hands, fall down and die, in the name of Jesus.
5. (Focus on one thing at a time. If you have any sickness on your body, lay your hands on the place and pray like this): O Lord, on this issue I need a miracle, in the name of Jesus.
6. (Focus your attention on another thing and pray aggressively like this): O Lord, on this issue I need a miracle, in the name of

Jesus.

7. Let my poverty disappear; let my prosperity appear, in the name of Jesus.

Chapter Five

How to Maintain Your Miracle

Every one of us needs a miracle at some time in our life! Every person alive on earth today has had trials and hardships. The devil would love for these trials to whittle at you, slowly but surely bringing you down to nothing, causing your life to be completely useless and hopeless. However, God has something marvelous and wonderful waiting for you!

I have good news for you! You don't have to live a defeated life. Miracle is readily available for every believer. You can make a choice today, right now as you are reading these words, to accept your miracle from God's hand. His desire and purpose for you is that you would be blessed.

How is that possible? "You may ask. In this booklet, I am going to give you vital information, wisdom that will turn your life around. You may feel defeated, alone, abandoned, or unloved; but I can assure you that's not the truth! There is one who has promised never to leave you or forsake you. God loves you and has a purpose and a plan for your life. He is waiting and willing to pour out from His bountiful storehouse of blessing, riches that are beyond your comprehension.

Carefully and prayerfully read this booklet. Drink in the words as a thirsty man in the desert would drink from the life- renewing, cool springs of an oasis.

Miracle and the Word of God

It's very important that you fill your life with the word of God. When you do, He will take that Word and touch it and make it real and powerful to you. The word is spirit and life; and within the word is the anointing. Therefore, storing the word in your heart allows God to transfer the anointing so you can use it in your life.

The greatest miracle that you'll ever receive is the new birth. Do you know Christians are born of a seed? It's true! 1 Peter 1:23 says, "Being born again, not of corruptible seed, but of incorruptible, by the word of God, which liveth and abideth forever."

Something that is corruptible will perish. Incorruptible means that something will not perish or fade; it will live on and on say Amen. When you were born again, you received the imperishable Word of life into your heart. The Word of God became the incorruptible seed that sealed your salvation. The Bible says everything else will pass away, but the Word of God will last forever.

You are a new creation in Christ and full of the life of God. All the old junk and trash of the past is dead and buried. People will notice when the incorruptible seed of the word of God begins to grow and change you into the likeness of Jesus Christ.

Perhaps you have only been a Christian a short time. One day you wake up, get in the car and it breaks down you get oil and grease on your hands trying to fix it, so you go into the bathroom to clean your hands. The bathroom sink plugs up, overflows, and ruins the carpet. You feel like a wreck and probably look like one too. You need a miracle! You want to believe God for one, but your faith seems to have vanished in the tangle of your situation. The problem here is that your mind hasn't been renewed by the word of truth.

Laying a strong foundation from God's Word is an essential element of receiving and maintaining your miracle. Speaking the words of Jesus, imitating Him in action, and staying focused on God (not your circumstance) will bring the miraculous and the means to maintain it. Christians have the seeds of miracles inside them because they have Jesus inside them. He is the word of God. (John 1:1 says, in the beginning was the word, and the word was with God, and the word was God). Since Jesus lives inside you, you also have the miracle of healing. Jesus in you will heal the surrounding situation. He is the miracle- giver and miracle-worker who will bring your miracle to reality.

Miracles Will Follow You

You don't have to allow the devil to ruin your life. If Jesus lives in you, so do miracles. No longer do seeds of doubt and fear have control over your life or destiny. In your mind and heart live the seeds of faith and miracles. They are growing in abundance. Soon you will harvest miracles by the bushel.

There can be miracles every place you go. Curses can be changed to blessing. Broken hearts can be healed. I don't care how hopeless the situation looks, a miracle can turn it around. Faith inside of you provides the potential for every miracle you will ever need!

If you've been healed, you need to maintain that healing. If the devil tries to bring disease to your body, you need to rebuke him! Stand firm on the living and powerful word of God. The Lord gives us wise instruction when He says, in (James 4:7) "Submit yourselves therefore to God. Resist the devil, and he will flee from you

Years ago I was sick, and recently the enemy tried to really hit me hard and bring it back into my body. I stood on the word, rebuked the devil, and the sickness has never come back —neither do I expect it to return. I had to maintain what I receive from the hand of God my healing.

God saved you, baptized you in the Holy Spirit, and healed you to be a "ye—ye" Christian-always going up and down – living by your feelings or circumstances. Live by faith, believing the promises of God, being filled with the Spirit and the Word.

God's Purpose for Miracles

God has a purpose in miracles. He doesn't say, "I think I will give you a miracle today." No, He wants to save you, heal you, and deliver you because He loves you, He cares for you, He loves you just as you are No matter where you are or what condition you're in –He loves you! Miracles prove Jesus is the son of God. John 10:36 -38 says, Say ye of him, whom the Father hath sanctified, and sent into the world, "Thou blasphemest; "because I said, I am the son of God? If I do not the works of my Father, believe me not. But if do, through ye believe not me, believe the works: that ye may know, and believe, that the Father is in me and I in Him. He said if you can't believe the words, believe the works.

I Love the word of God, and I believe the works that go with it. Seeing the miraculous at work proves that He is the real, living Son of God. Telling people that God has answered your prayer will attract them. No one wants to hear about a dead god, religious rituals, or something that will not meet their need. People want to hear about a living God who loves them and will take care of them. Since

He loves and cares for you, He will touch you and do the miraculous. The miraculous draws people to hear the gospel. The power and anointing of the Lord attracts people. If you move and operate in the anointing, your miracle will help draw others to the Lord.

He Is Risen!

Miracles prove that Jesus rose from the dead. A dead man doesn't heal the sick. Jesus is alive now, and that is why you can expect your miracle He is seated at the right hand of the Father in heaven with power and majesty; and He is able to deliver you!

What can you do to stay close to God? I've asked people that question and they respond, read the Word, pray, fast, tithe, rarely do people reply, Attend church; however, if you don't get in church and stay in church, you won't maintain what you have received. If you have a problem, the body of believers at your church will help you stay strong and maintain the right course with the Lord. When you are around people who are anointed, the strength of their anointing will join with yours. That united, powerful force can move obstacles, tear down barriers, and help you keep what you have received from God's hand. There's anointing available in the Body of Jesus Christ. The more anointing we get, the more we'll be changed. The anointing will cause you to stand steadfast, unmovable, always abounding in work of the Lord (see 1 Corinthians 15:58).

The enemy doesn't want you to be committed to church. He knows if you are, you'll grow then you will be a threat to him and his demonic forces. Satan has many ways to distract you from going to church. He will let something happen that causes you to become offended in small ways- the worship is too loud, or it's not loud enough, they don't show enough attention, or they are overly friendly. These offenses could keep you out of church, causing you to lose your miracle. You need to attend church to maintain your miracle.

How to Maintain Your Miracle

Whenever Jesus healed, He provided a "miracle maintenance" program. He followed the miracle with instructions and counsel on what to do after the healing was manifested.

Obey the word:

After the leper was healed in Matthew 8:4, Jesus told him, "go thy way, show thyself to the priest, and offer the gift that Moses commanded, for a testimony unto them." In Luke 5:14 Jesus told the leper, "offer for thy cleansing, according as Moses commanded" What did He tell the leper? He told him to go and do what the word said to do when leprosy was healed. Jesus pointed the leper to the word of God. To maintain your miracle you must read your Bible. Read the word, keep the Word, and keep in the word, stay in the word for there is life in the word of God.

Quit sinning:

In the gospel of Mark, Jesus showed us something else that's very important for maintaining miracle. Some men had a friend who was paralyzed. They had heard about the miracles of Jesus and knew if they could only get their friend to Him, he would be healed. Unfortunately, there were so many people surrounding the home where Jesus was teaching that they had to find an alternate plan to get close to Him.

Climbing the stairs to the roof, while carefully balancing their friend on his stretcher, they made a hole in the roof to let the paralytic down to Jesus.

Once that was accomplished, Jesus told the man that his sins were forgiven, and the paralysis was healed immediately.

If you want to maintain your miracle and your healing, you must stop sinning. Live a holy life, walk in integrity, and don't compromise or make excuses for yourself. Follow Jesus. He is your pattern and example. Don't imitate other people. Once you have received your miracle, you need to exhibit a lifestyle in accordance with what God says in His word about living for Him.

If you persist in sin, you may lose the anointing and miss out with God Don't blame the church or other people for the way you behave. Take responsibility for what you do. Stop sinning. God in His word. He knows that we have a tendency to sin-miss the mark. In (1 John 1:9) the apostle John declares, if we confess our sins, he is faithful and just and will forgive us our sins and purify us from all unrighteousness.

There is no sin so great that God cannot cleanse it. He has provided the precious blood of His Son, Jesus Christ, to wash away every stain, blemish, and spot. When we turn to God's immeasurable supply of mercy and forgiveness in repentance, He will remove our sins far from us; as far as the east is from the west. Our fellowship with Him is then restored and we can rest in the knowledge that He never stopped loving us but was always waiting, with open arms, for us to come back into His presence. Praise God.

Tell people what God has done for you.

In Mark 5:19, Jesus told the demoniac. Go home to thy friends, and tell them how great things the Lord have done for thee, and have had compassion on thee. One of the best ways to maintain a miracle is to talk about it. Let people know what God does for you and your family you'll not only maintain your miracle, you'll get more. Once you make a breakthrough, God will manifest His power in your life by leaps and bounds.

Take care of your body.

A young girl's parents were given important instructions in Mark 5:43 and he commanded that something should be given her to eat. Do you know that Jesus wants you to take care of your body?

When I minister, I get tired. Sometimes my schedule is very busy. I have found that there are some practical ways to maintain your miracle. Take care of your body; eat healthy, nutritious food get plenty of rest; take a break. God made your body, and He knows that you need sleep and eat.

How You Can Help Others Maintain Their Miracle

A young man went to Socrates and asked him how he could get wisdom. They went down to the ocean and Socrates began to dunk the man beneath the waves. When he emerged from the water gulping for air, Socrates asked him what he wanted. "Wisdom," he gasped. The scene was repeated several times with the same resulting answer from the would–be seeker. The fourth time the lad had a different answer, Air Socrates told him, When you want wisdom as much as you want air, then you'll get it.

Get hungry for God

Are you as hungry for God as you are for air? When you can't get enough of His Presence, His Word, Prayer, and fellowship with other believes, then you'll be in a position to maintain your miracle from God. What should you do to help those around you who get saved, Spirit – filled, or healed to maintain God's best for them?

Encourage them to stay in fellowship.

Let them know that they are an important part of the fellowship.

Get them into the word by making them accountable.

A leader came to me one day and told me he liked to pray and do other things but he didn't read his Bible on a consistent basis. I told him I would hold him responsible by checking on him once a week and I did. He got a Bible-reading plan and started to read the word. Eventually, he called me and said he was doing so well reading the Bible without supervision, that I didn't have to check on him any longer.

Pray for them and with them.

When people are going through hard time, get with them and pray. Praying with them will be more effective than simply praying for them.

Lead others into the blessing and

responsibility of giving.

People need to know God desires that we give of ourselves and give of our finances. Obedience is one of the keys to maintaining your miracle from God. If you say, I love Jesus, but you don't obey what He says, then it's time to examine where you are in your relationship with God. People can say they love the Lord, but they need to follow His commands.

To maintain the miraculous, you can't leave anything out. Life in the Spirit is not a happy experience all the time. Don't expect to coast along in your Christian life without doing what God desires. Read the word. Pray. Witness. Stay in the anointing. Soak up the Spirit. Laugh in the Spirit. All of these are important to the maintenance of your miracle from the new birth until the end of the race when God calls you to His side.

Miracle Maintenance Scriptures

Thy word have I hid in mine heart, that I might not sin against thee. Blessed art thou, O LORD: teach me thy statutes" (Psalms 9:11-12).

No weapon that is formed against thee shall prosper; and every tongue that shall rise against thee in judgment thou shalt condemn. This is the heritage of the servants of the LORD, and their righteousness is of me, saith the LORD. (Isaiah 54:170).

Therefore I say unto you, what things so ever ye desire, when ye pray, believe that ye receive them, and ye shall have them" (Mark 11:24).

The Price of Miracle

Sally was only eight years old when she heard Mommy and Daddy talking about her little brother, George. He was very sick and they had done everything they could afford to save his life. Only a very expensive surgery could help him now…and that was out of the financial question. She heard Daddy say it with a whispered desperation, "Only a miracle can save him now." Sally went to her bedroom and pulled her piggybank from its hiding place in the closet. She shook all the change out on the floor and counted it carefully. Tying the coins up in a cold-weather-kerchief, she slipped out of the apartment and made her way to the corner drug store….

"And what do you want?" The pharmacist asked in an annoyed tone of voice. "Well, I want to talk to you about my brother, he's sick… and I want to buy a miracle." "I beg your pardon," said the pharmacist. "My Daddy says only a miracle can save him now.... so how much does a miracle cost?" "We don't sell miracles here, little girl. I can't help you."

"Listen, I have the money to pay for it. Just tell me how much it costs?" The well-dressed man who was talking with the pharmacist stooped down and asked, "What kind of a miracle does your brother need?" "I don't know," Sally answered. A tear started down her cheek. "I just know he's really sick and Mommy says he needs an operation. But my folks can't pay for it... so I have money. "How much do you have?" asked the well-dressed man.

"A dollar and eleven cents," Sally answered proudly. "And it's all the money I have in the world."

"Well, what a coincidence," smiled the well-dressed man. A dollar and eleven cents....the exact price of a miracle to save a little brother." He took her money in one hand and with the other hand he grasped her mitten and said "Take me to where you live. I want to see your brother and meet your parents."

That well-dressed man was Dr. Carlton Armstrong, renowned surgeon... specializing in solving George's malady. The operation was completed.... without charge and it wasn't long until George was home again and doing well.

Sally smiled to herself. She knew exactly how much a miracle cost... one dollar and eleven cents... plus the faith of a little child! How old is your faith? Think about it and remain blessed.

Chapter Six

When the Heavens Become Brass

The message of this week is for those who believe in the God of the suddenlies, those who know that no matter how fast the enemy has been running; just a word from the Master is enough to halt his race. After all, in the beginning, when the earth was without form and void all that was required to bring sanity was for the voice of the Lord to say, "Let there be light," and there was light. Also, when there was satanic storm on the sea, all that was required to quench it was for the voice of the Lord to say, "Peace be still."

The message is entitled "When the heavens become brass." Let us start from the book of Genesis, from the first man to see an open heaven. In Genesis 28:11-12 we see Jacob as a very confused man. The Scripture says, "And he lighted upon a certain place and tarried there all night, because the sun was set; and he took of the stones of that place, and put them for his pillows, and lay down in that place to sleep. (His head was on the stone. When his head got on the stone, then his vision became clear. That stone was Jesus). And he dreamed, and beholds a ladder set up on the earth and the top of it reached to heaven: and behold the angels of God ascending and descending. And behold the Lord stood above it, and said, I am the Lord God of Abraham thy father, and the God of Isaac: the land wherein thou liest, to thee will I give it, and to thy seed." Right from this experience, the life of Jacob never remained the same.

You need an open heaven. When this man saw an open heavens, for the first time he saw a ladder going right into the heavenlies, and God was there talking to him for the first time in his life. If you need to do seven days dry fast or to go on only water for 21 days for God to speak to you for five minutes, it 's worth it, because if God talks to you for two minutes, it is better than a preacher talking to you for ten hours. If God talks to you for one hour, it is better for you than a preacher talking to you the whole of your life. When you have open heavens you will hear the voice of the Lord.

Deuteronomy 28:23: "And thy heavens that are over thy head shall be brass, and the earth under thee shall be iron. The Lord shall make the rain of thy land powder and dust: from heaven shall it come down upon thee, until thou be destroyed."

Please, pray like this: "My heavens shall not become brass, in the name of Jesus."

That Scripture tells us that the heaven over a particular person's head can become brass, and the earth under his feet can become iron. It is a terrible situation when the heavens become brass. This means that God has allocated to everybody an air space above his head, which can either be open or can become brass.

Matthew 3:13-16 says, "Then cometh Jesus from Galilee to Jordan unto John, to be baptized of him. But John forbad him, saying, I have need to be baptized of thee, and comest thou to me? And Jesus answering said unto him, Suffer it to be so now: for thus it becometh us to fulfill all righteousness: then he suffered him. And Jesus, when he was baptized, went up straightway out of the water: and, lo, the heavens were opened unto him..." That passage says "Him" and not all those people standing around. John the Baptist saw the Spirit of God descending like a dove; and lighting upon Him. Jesus did not go out to minister until He received open heavens. He could not operate because when the Old Testament closed at Malachi, for 400 years God did not send any prophet and did not talk to anybody, the heaven was brass. It had to be opened before the Son of God could start His ministration.

In John 1:51, it is written, "And he saith unto him, verily, verily, I say unto you, hereafter ye shall see heaven open, and the angels of God ascending and descending upon the Son of man." They first of all ascend and then descend, meaning that the initiative for the angels of God to come and help you lies with you. The initiative has to come from the earth.

For your life to prosper, the heavens must be involved, because the heaven above us is seeing everything. If a man is ever going to prosper, he cannot do it outside of heaven. A destiny remains stagnant until a connection is made between earth and heaven. On your own, you can't do anything. Even those who don't believe that God exists and don't serve the Lord are existing by the mercy of God. God sends His grace on the evil and on the good. Even if you said He does not exist, no problem; but the fact that you are alive shows that you are enjoying His mercies.

A destiny remains in the same place until a connection between heaven and earth is made, as with the ladder in the case of Jacob. You must have a process or a procedure to bring heaven to earth, or to join the earth to heaven. Until your heavens are opened, you cannot even locate your ladder, let alone go anywhere. Some people have broken ladders, some have no ladder at all, and that is why they have never in their lives seen anything positive coming from heaven. Until your heavens open, you don't really know how sweet God could be. But when the heavens open, you know and experience the power of God. He will speak with you, you will hear that voice which many prophets have heard, and their lives never remained the same. God cannot speak to you and you will remain as you are. There must be a connection between earth and heaven. But when this heaven becomes brass over somebody's head, his destiny is as good as dead.

Seven Major Things That Happen In The Heavenliness

There are seven major things that happen in the heavenliness above. Ephesians 1:3 says, "Blessed be the God and Father of our Lord Jesus Christ, who hath blessed us with all spiritual blessings in heavenly places in Christ."

The heavenliness is the location of spiritual blessings.

The heavenliness is the headquarters of darkness. In Daniel 10, we find that for 21 days the heaven was brass. Why? There was a prince of Persia up there holding tight the angel bringing an answer to Daniel's prayer. He could not bring the answer until he wrestled with the prince for 21 days. For all those 21 days, the heaven was brass because nothing was coming through. Until Angel Michael came and cleared that demon out of the skies, Daniel did not get his answer. This means that prayers can be hindered by the headquarters of darkness above. When the whole of heavenlies are occupied by darkness in the life of a person, the person cannot receive the rain of God. Such a situation describes what is meant by the heavens becoming brass.

The heavens are the battlefield for spiritual warfare. Ephesians 6:12 says, "For we wrestle not against flesh and blood, but against principalities, against powers, against the rulers of darkness of this world, against wickedness in high places."

The heavens are the sphere or the arena of angelic activities. Ephesians 3:10 says, "To the intent that now unto the principalities and powers in heavenly places might be known by the church the manifold wisdom of God." When you say, "I bind, I loose, I bind, I loose" and the heavens do not answer you, you are wasting your time.

The heavenlies are the battleground of the success of our Lord Jesus Christ in spiritual warfare. Psalm 103:19 says, "The Lord hath prepared His throne in the heavens: and His kingdom ruleth over all."

The heavens now are the location of believers' position in Christ. Ephesians 2:6 says, "And hath raised us up together, and made us sit together in heavenly places in Christ Jesus." That is where we are supposed to be ruling from but we are not there. This is why the enemy is boasting.

The heavenlies are the action field of the triangular powers. What are the triangular powers? They are the sun, the moon and the stars. That's why God says, "The sun shall not smite thee by day or the moon by night."

When you look at these seven things, you will begin to understand that if all spiritual blessings are in the heavenlies, and one way or the other, they are not coming down; it means that the heavens have become brass. Since the heavens are the battlefield for spiritual warfare, if a person loses all the battle fought there, then the heavens have become brass for him. If the heaven is the arena of angelic activities, and the angels do not come to assist you, your heaven has become brass. No wonder Jacob saw them ascending and descending. If the heaven is your location in Christ, and you are not sitting there, it has become brass, a hard metal.

We need to pray some brass-destroying, brass-shattering prayers. When you notice that there is silence from heaven, you get no information, those who want to help you get into trouble themselves, you go to borrow money and discover that the man who wants to give you the money has been involved in an accident and everywhere seems blocked, you have to check the condition of your heavens.

At this juncture, I would like you to pray like this:

You forces of brassy heavens, give way by fire, in the name of Jesus.

You heavens of brass, shatter, in the name of Jesus.

Whatsoever that is making the sky to thicken over my head, die, in the name of Jesus.

Iron and Brass

Iron and brass in the spirit are equivalent to famine, dryness and drought. It is this dry and arid land that the devil normally rules. The Bible says, "When an unclean spirit has left a man, it roams around in dry places, i.e. in the lives of those that the heavens have closed. That is what the Bible means by dry places. When the heavens are closed over the head of a person, there would be traffic of demons in the life of that person. So, the questions that are pertinent to ask are: "Are your heavens open or closed? Are you really concerned about your life, progress, calling and destiny?" Once you are concerned about your life, your progress, calling and destiny are the first things to check to know whether your heavens are closed or not. If your heavens are closed and have become brass, demons would overcome you with ease. Nothing will go smoothly. Everything will be so hard, the ground will become very dry and plantations will not survive. Sometimes when you go into a house to pray and say, "Father, in the name of Jesus," you would continue to pray and it will flow and appear as if you should not stop. But when you go to some houses and say, "Father, in the name of Jesus," the people there would be falling asleep. As you pray you would notice that something is pushing the prayer back into your mind.

Sometimes ago, some brethren and I went to pray for a sister who was very ill. As we began to pray, I felt a thick darkness. I opened my eyes and said, "Madam, what are you doing here?" She said, "Em, before my father died, he willed the house to us, the children, and as the eldest daughter, I am staying here." I said, "Do you want to die?" She said, "No." I said, "But you have your own house, why are you not living there?" She said, "I've given it out to tenants." The heavens closed over that place.

When the heavens are closed and there is no rain, plantations will not survive. When the heavens are closed, seeds are wasted because when they are put in the soil, they will not grow. You will plant much but reap very little because the heavens are closed and the whole of life is a struggle. There is a lot of profitless hard work. One man was in Germany for 13 years and couldn't get one single certificate. To worsen his case, his father, who was a herbalist, used charms to summon him home. He suddenly packed his things and left Germany, and all of a sudden he discovered that he was at Muritala Mohammed Airport, Lagos. It was then his eyes cleared and he said, "What am I doing here?" They took him back to his hometown. He is now a herbalist like his father. The heavens closed.

When the heavens are closed, you need more laborers to do a very little job. Many people will be there struggling. When the heavens have become brass that is when worldliness and sins find their way into the lives of Christians. When the heavens become brass, problem remain the same even after deliverance ministration, a person will consume much more than he can produce or contribute, debt would be rising and the income would be low. When the heavens have become brass, a person will be laboring on hard ground. He will labor and sweat so much and achieve very little. You know that when the ground is dry, and a farmer is hoeing, the hoe would be making much noise on the ground but would be making little progress. When the heavens become brass devourers are released unto a person's labor. It leads to deflected and paralyzed life, and the affected person would notice that his spiritual life is going down.

It is possible that the heavens of somebody were open before but are closed now, and the person is now living on old and past achievements. The person does not have fresh fire and his prayers have become ordinary noise. His mind wanders about during prayers and Bible reading becomes a religion. He no longer derives any benefits from Bible studies and he goes to a great length to spiritualize the foolishness that he is practicing. Unbelievers boldly toss him to and fro.

When the heavens are closed, the person finds it very easy to co-exist with darkness. When you find it easy to co-exist with darkness, it is a sign of brassy heavens. When the heavens of a person become brass his prayer life becomes vague and powerless; the joy of the Lord no longer remains his strength.

Beloved, do you know of certainty the condition of the heavens over your head? This is a very important question. Before you start blaming anybody for your problems, first ask yourself this question; "Are my heavens open?" Check that thoroughly, look deeply into your heart, look deeply into your life and your commitment to Jesus. Have you noticed, beloved, that you sow much but bring in little? What is the sense in working so hard and at the end of the day, you go to the bank to cash money and behind you are armed robbers? This is the money you have sweated for years. Do you eat fatty things and become lean? Are your expectations cut short most of the time? Do you look for much from your investment but very little comes in? Do you have leakages in your purse? Do you have a bag with holes so that nothing is retained? Do you come to the house of God and the word of God becomes dry and empty to you? Do you notice a strong dominion over you life? Then you have work to do.

I heard something from a certain man that troubled and challenged me. He said that spiritually, you deserve what you tolerate. If you allow evil powers to drink your blood, they will drink it. If you allow your heavens to be closed, it shall be closed. When the heavens have become brass, that is when some people who have no money would begin to sing, "When I get home, when I get home, my sorrows shall be over." That is not correct. The Bible says, "Verily, I say unto you, there is no man that has left house, parents, brethren, wife, children for the kingdom of God's sake, who shall not receive manifold blessings, even this present time and in the world to come."

If you want God to change you, you have an opportunity. If you say, "Well, I refuse to tolerate brassy heavens," then it shall be so and you shall not tolerate it and your heavens shall be opened.

When the heavens are closed, and it has become brass, the wealth of a person goes to the wrong hands. The person's child becomes sick, and there would be no money to treat the child. The poor child is exposed to mosquito bite because there is no money to buy insecticide. It is a sign of brassy heaven. If you tolerate it, it will continue. When you find that everything is just slipping away from your hands, this will come and will go away, another will come and go away, check the condition of your heavens. Many sicknesses come upon people who are not eating well. When the heavens become brass, people feed poorly. Proverb 10:15 says, "The rich man's wealth is his strong city, the destruction of the poor is their poverty." When the heavens are closed, scarcity is created in the midst of plenty. When heavens are closed, the person will pay his tithe to the wrong place. If you refuse to pay it to God, something else will collect it from you. But when the heavens are opened unto you, the devourers would be silenced. There was a brother who whenever he got his salary, used it to settle debts. He never paid anything to God. One day, something happened. He soaked his choicest clothes in the water and went into the house to bring soap. By the time he came back, both the bucket and the clothes had been stolen. He shouted, screamed and did everything, but nothing worked for him until he began to pay his tithe to God.

It does not pay to cheat God because you will just end up closing the whole of the heavenlies. One of the greatest things that could happen to a man is to have open heavens. And I pray that the Lord will give you open heavens today, in the name of Jesus. When you have open heavens, blessings are released unto you in abundance and you will take the good treasure of the land where the Lord has planted you. But if you continue to live in disobedience, the heavens would remain closed.

How to Destroy Brass in the Heavens

Repent from any sin that has closed the heavens against you: This is the first thing to do. Disobedience and sin will close the heavens.

Pray brass-shattering prayers: There are some prayers that will do that for you and there are some prayers that cannot do it.

Engage in sacrificial giving: Give to God in a way that you will feel that you have given something. You should give to God sacrificially, generously, unselfishly, cheerfully and without grudge. You should give proportionately, you should give at every opportunity that God asks you to give. You give without open show. The Bible says, "If you bring your tithes to my house, I will open the windows of heaven." What the Bible is telling you is that, if you do not bring it those windows shall be closed and devourers shall be released.

Long sessions of praises: Take time to learn worship songs. Take time to learn hymns in the hymn books. Spend quality time praising God. Sometimes don't even pray at all, just praise Him. Long sessions of praises break the heavenlies open.

Destroy ancestral covenants and altars: Please, pray like this: "Every ancestral altar of destiny destruction, die, in the name of Jesus.

Drop all languages of closed heavens: The languages of closed heavens are for example, "What gonna be gonna be. What goes up must come down. What's gonna be gonna be and there is nothing you can do about it." When you say that what is going to happen, must happen and that there is nothing anybody can do about it, you are speaking the language of closed heavens. There is one demonic Yoruba proverb of laziness and backwardness that says, "If it is not possible to go forward, go backward," whereas the Bible says, "Go forward!" The languages of closed heavens include, "Eh, I've prayed and prayed and fasted and nothing has happened. Everything is upside down." Drop such statements for you are making yourself miserable. Nobody can make you miserable unless you permit the person to do so. A person can stand in front of you and abuse you from morning till night, but if you make up your mind inside that you will not allow what he is saying to make you miserable, you will not be miserable. If you live with a person and the person does not appreciate what you are doing and whatever you do is wrong, if you allow it to get to you, you will become miserable. But if you decide that whatever he is saying will not get to you, you'll not be miserable. So, you can choose to be miserable or not to be. The choice is yours.

You can also choose what to say. You may decide to speak the language of heaven or speak the language of hell fire. Saying, "I'm fed up with all these," is the language of closed heavens. When you say that you are fed up, the devil will say, "Yes you are fed up." When you say, "I'm fed up with this marriage, let us pack up everything," the devil would say, "Yes, and pack it up." You speak the language of closed heavens when you say, "Eh, God cannot do it." When somebody says, "I am frustrated in this situation, I will stop coming to church, Lord what is my sin that you are doing all these to me, or are you saying that you are for some special people?" It is the language of closed heaven. If you have been uttering those kinds of statements maybe not verbally, even in your heart, it is still a voice of closed heavens. You must stop saying them and repent of them.

PRAYER POINTS
1. My heavens, open by fire, in the name of Jesus.
2. You my enemies, you shall not prevail, in the name of Jesus.
   - God, arise in my life and let the world know that you are my God, in the name of Jesus.
3. My hidden riches, be revealed and be released, in the name of Jesus.
   - windows of heavens, open unto my life, in the name of Jesus.
4. Satanic brass of iron working against me, shatter, in the name of Jesus.
5. Sun, moon and stars, refuse to co-operate with my enemies, in the name of Jesus.
6. Every power that has been assigned to sit on my breakthrough, die, in the name of Jesus.

7. Every Pharaoh from my home town, sink in the Red Sea, in the name of Jesus.

Chapter Seven

Wrestling with Shadows

This message is very important, especially to those who were born and brought up in this environment. Life is something many people fail to understand because there are so many questions those men cannot answer. For example, Cain and Abel were two men born of the same parents. They had similar backgrounds, similar abilities and were headed in the same direction but Abel was successful while Cain was overshadowed by failure and frustration. The world is exactly like that.

A lot of black people are wrestling with shadows. What does this mean? Some people have done all there is to do for them to be successful, yet they remain failures. Some even have higher degrees and have done everything that qualifies one for resounding success yet success remains elusive; their children are disobedient, their marriages are unstable and sicknesses are becoming a routine affair. A person just discovers that in one particular area or in many areas of his life, he is struggling with something he cannot understand or identify. He just goes from one problem to another. He is always at the edge of good health but never really achieving good health. Sometimes the way may look clear once in a while but as some people try to go to the clear way, they stumble and fall. This is what we call wrestling with shadows. Many people cannot get a grip of what is happening. They are struggling with something they cannot understand or identify.

We are in a world of powerful forces that harass men. These powerful forces do not operate according to natural laws. There is a lamentation on this in the book of Ecclesiastes. Ecclesiastes 9: 11 says, "I returned, and I saw under the sun, that the race is not to the swift, nor the battle to the strong, neither yet bread to the wise, nor yet riches to men of understanding, nor yet favor to men of skill; but time and chance happeneth to them all." This lamentation proves that there are forces operating on the lives of men that men cannot understand. The forces that determine the course of our lives are both visible and invisible. The powers that confuse the lives of men most can do so through what we call the mouth gate. A lot of people are in such bondage. 1 Corinthians 10:16 talks about the kind of communion we have in the church now. It says, "The cup of blessing which we bless, is it not the communion of the blood of Christ? The bread which we break, is it not the communion of the body of Christ?" During communion service, when the cup and the bread have been blessed, the cup then has the power to transmit the blessings of the New Covenant to those who drink it. Therefore, by simple spiritual interpretation, it shows that a physical object like a cup used during the Last Supper can transmit spiritual power.

Likewise in Numbers chapter 5, we read about what happens when a woman is suspected of being unfaithful to her marriage vows in those days. Numbers 5: 18 says, "And the priest shall set the woman before the Lord, and uncover the woman's head, and put the offering of memorial in her hands, which is the jealousy offering. And the priest shall have in his hand the bitter water that caused the curse." (They would have water inside a cup and issue a curse on the water). Verses 19 - 22 say, "And the priest shall charge her by an oath, and say unto the woman, if no man has lain with thee, and if thou hast not gone aside to uncleanness with another instead of thy husband, be thou free from this bitter water that causeth the curse. But if thou hast gone aside unto another instead of thy husband, and if thou be defiled, and some man have lain with thee beside thine husband.

Then the priest shall charge the woman with an oath of cursing, and the priest shall say unto the woman, The Lord make thee a curse and an oath among thy people, when the Lord doth make thy thigh to rot, and thy belly to swell. And this water that causeth the curse shall go into thy bowels, to make thy belly to swell, and thy thigh to rot. And the woman shall say, Amen, amen." In this case, the cup of water is the vehicle through which the destroying power is transmitted. So, if the woman had been truly unfaithful, that water would transmit the curse and the belly would swell and explode. So, destroying powers can be transferred by physical objects. Therefore, if you have been served meals from the devil's table, you may live your life wrestling with shadows unless you are purged. Once you get something from the table of the devil you would be wrestling with shadows and won't know what you are fighting against unless you are purged. The reason is that what you are fighting against is inside your body and you are thinking that it is one old woman or one relative somewhere. The thing has already been deposited inside, and you are going around with it.

In our environment, wicked people succeed in making some people to be wrestling with shadows through the mouth gate. Sometime ago, I went to somebody's office and the person said, "You are welcome. We have some meat that we just used for a festival." I said, "What do I do with it?" He said, "It is for consumption." I said, "I don't eat food from the table of the devil." He said, "What? Table of the devil?" I said, "Jesus has been made a once and for all sacrifice. Anybody that is killing anything after Jesus died is sacrificing to the devil and those who eat it are eating from the table of the devil." The scripture is very clear on this. It can be very frustrating when somebody is fighting an external force when the problem is internal. It can also be very frustrating when somebody has a physical object in his possession, which is the vehicle of his problem and he does not know. Sometime ago, we prayed for a sister and the demon spirit that spoke from her said, "Well, ask her to bring the cloth we gave to her." The sister brought the cloth, which was destroyed before she could regain her freedom. It means that as long as she had that cloth in her possession, she could sing all the praise worship in this planet, and read all the psalms, but there would be no freedom.

Sometime ago, we held a revival service in a church and when an altar call was made to those who wanted to receive the baptism of the Holy Spirit, I saw a dear old woman who came crying and saying that she could not understand why it was difficult for her to receive the baptism even after many revivalists had visited her church. So, I said, "Madam, you will be filled with the power today." She said, "Thank you my son I will try." I told her to pray and she prayed until she was sweating. Her clothes were soaked. I was impressed with her prayers yet nothing happened. I could get impressed but I am not the giver of the Holy Spirit. At a stage, I left her alone and sat somewhere else to pray. I asked the Lord what was wrong with her and the Lord said I should look at her hand. I looked at her hand and saw a particular ring on her fourth finger. On the ring was the symbol of a half moon. The

Lord said that with that ring on her finger, His Spirit would not enter into her life. Then I said, "Mama, open your eyes. Who gave you this ring?" She told me that she inherited it from her great grandmother. I took the ring from her and made her to understand that the half moon was the sign of witchcraft. She gladly gave it to me and did not have to pray for one minute before she received the power of the Holy Ghost. She did not know that her enemy was on her fourth finger for 25 years. She slept with it, woke up with it, bathed with it, went everywhere and did everything with it. So, she was busy wrestling with shadows instead of the real thing, which was on her fourth finger.

When you are wrestling with shadows, you would be kept away from receiving the blessings of God. God would be offering the blessings but you would not be able to get them. Sometimes you may not even realize that there is a blessing to receive. Somebody who is under witchcraft attack in our environment would be manipulated, intimidated and dominated. What do I mean by manipulation? The following illustration gives us the answer. Sometime ago, a man married a very beautiful wife, who was light in complexion. But he noticed that in the afternoons, the woman would take a knife and begin to scratch her body and salt would be coming out of her body. He got worried and decided to visit a white garment prophet. Before he got to the white garment prophet, the woman had visited the white garment prophet to inform him that her husband was coming and that he should charge him very high fees. They were members of the same evil society but the man did not know. That is manipulation. How can you have a bed in your house and somebody would tell you to be sleeping on the mat, or they remove your all the protein food from your diet, that is domination and intimidation. The wife of a man asked him for soup money and he had only $20. He gave her the $20 and she took it, tore it up and said, "What do you want me to do with $20?" And the man slapped her. The woman said, "Okay, you have just slapped yourself." Right from that day, the man started feeling as if somebody was whipping him. Even when he was in the office, it was the same thing. He would be dancing in the streets and people thought he was mad. He was in that condition until he got to a prayer meeting where the Lord sent fire on the invisible evil whip. The man was wrestling with what we call shadows. In normal wrestling matches, what we have is a physical challenge. But when your challenger is a shadow, you have an impossible task in your hands.

How Do People Get To Wrestle With Shadows?

Idol worship: Worship and acknowledgement of false gods would lead somebody to wrestle with shadows. Involvement with dark societies and occult powers would cause a person to wrestle with shadows. If somebody's father was a secret cult member, he would be wrestling with shadows.

Disobedience: Disobedience to God's clear command would lead to wrestling with shadows. The Bible says that at the time of ignorance, God winked at it. But if you understand it and you are disobedient to it, you are inviting shadows.

Disrespect for parents and the elderly: This makes people to wrestle with shadows.

Sexual perversion: All forms of sexual perversion, as far as the Bible is concerned, make people to wrestle with shadows.

Stealing: All kinds of stealing and also being stingy with God make people to wrestle with shadows.

Curses: Anyone operating under a curse would be wrestling with shadows.

Remote control forces: There are some forces

called remote control forces. Somebody who lives in London could be remote controlling the life of another person in Nigeria like somebody operating a television set. Our environment is so filled with wickedness that many people are already programd to spend the better part of their lives wrestling with shadows. This message gives you have an opportunity to strike back and recover your blessings.

Six Areas By Which Dark Powers Make People In This Environment To Wrestle With Shadows

Attack by demon idols: The first area by which they make people in this environment to wrestle with shadows is what I call attack by demon idols. They send a demon idol to a person to attack him or her. They cut off part of people's clothes, steal their shoes or underwear's or collect things from people's body such as their hair, nail, etc and give them to the demon idol to enable it to identify who to fight. If you lose things like that, and wave it off as one of those things, you will be surprised to find that it is not one of those things, but an attack. These demon idols which are usually short come with big clubs in their hands. They are generally used to kill or render people useless. I know a person who was attacked with a demon idol. The thing came into his bedroom and hit him on the right hand with its club. The hand got paralyzed immediately. If not for the fact that he knew the name of Jesus, he would have been maimed in that hand for life. A person who is spiritually blind would not be able to see a demon idol. So, if it is sent to attack such a person, he or she will not know what hit him or her. If you allow them to go free, you are giving them opportunity to stage a comeback. So, you must deal with them.

Way Out

Withdraw your stolen materials or the parts cut off from your body from them.

Issue an invitation to the demon idol to come by the authority of the Lord Jesus Christ and command it to go back to the sender.

Command the evil materials that have been injected into your system to be neutralized by the blood of Jesus. That is how to handle them.

If you are living in a flat where a demon idol has walked through before, whether it succeeded or not in its assignment in that place, something has already been deposited there, so, you need to clean up the place.

Strange touch: A strange touch is when you feel that somebody touched you but you did not see the person or even if you saw the person, certain things began to go wrong as from that moment. That is what is called a strange touch. When somebody with a spiritual poison in his hand shakes your hand or touches any part of your body, you would feel serious heat internally or a funny sensation. That is a strange touch. Life would become meaningless as from that moment.

Way Out

Shake off the strange touch, in Jesus' name.

Ask for the fire of the Holy Spirit to saturate every organ of your body.

Return the strange touch to the sender.

Beloved, if you notice that someone is just looking for an opportunity to touch you, you better beware. Women who do not mind men touching parts of their bodies carelessly are playing with fire. They can receive a strange touch through that way. A believer ought to angrily give such men a stern warning, plead the blood of Jesus and shake off the evil touch. It may be the touch of wastage, which can result into all kinds of female problems like late marriage, bareness, etc.

Encounter with the spirit of death: Wicked people can send the spirit of death to a person. This evil spirit is generally a dark tall shadow. It walks into the room and wants to touch the person. Or the person could be seeing another personality inside him or he could be seeing coffins, or he could be seeing himself being buried, or he could see people planning his funeral. Another evidence of the spirit of death pursing somebody is when you have masquerades running after you in the dream. A lot of people have this encounter.

Way Out

Bind the spirit of death and hell.

Return spiritual obituary to the senders.

Keep declaring Psalm 118: 17 which says, "I shall not die, but live and declare the works of the Lord." If you have experienced this kind of thing before and you did not cancel it, you maybe walking about the street three-quarter dead by now.

Strange call: Some people have heard their names called out in the middle of a sleep, these are strange calls. Sometimes, a person could hear a familiar voice call out his name three times. If the person answers, he or she becomes a shadow fighter as from that day. A lot of people have answered such strange calls. Many times they call us like that but God just does not allow us to hear it. He sends them back before we even have time to hear because He says, "Touch not my anointed and do my prophets no harm."

Way Out

Ask for forgiveness for not being a proper sheep of Jesus, because He says, "My sheep know my voice and a stranger they will not follow." If then as a child of God, you heard a strange voice and you answered, it means that something is wrong with your spiritual life. So, the first thing is to ask for forgiveness for answering the call that is not from Jesus.

Rewind the call.

Return the call back to the sender. If you had answered, withdraw your answer by this simple prayer: I withdraw the answer, in Jesus' name.

Serpentine spirits attack: Serpentine spirits are very dangerous demons. They represent the dragon we read about in Revelation 12. A person under serpentine attack may be pursued by a snake in the dream. A snake may spit on the person or bite the person. The person may be playing and discussing with a snake in the dream. What are the implications of all these? They would prevent the person from achieving goodness in life. They would scare the person away from good things. If the person has received saliva from the snake, he would have an evil mark on him. But the blood of Jesus can rub it off. If a snake has bitten the person then spiritual poison has been released into his or her body. This would cause sickness and death in the person's life. The snake venom that has been spiritually introduced into a person's life can amputate the person's spiritual life. If somebody plays and discusses with a snake in the dream, it means that he or she has a covenant with the snake and water spirit as well. The person may be unconscious of this.

Way Out

Rebuke the serpentine spirit, in Jesus' name.

Withdraw your name from their register because they just don't send the snake to anybody. They have a book from which they consult.

Plead the blood of Jesus and ask the Holy Spirit to neutralize the serpentine saliva and every poison injected into your body.

Release yourself from every conscious and unconscious serpentine covenant. Now you can command any obstruction to leave your way. If a snake is running after somebody in the dream, the truth is that the snake is trying to chase the person away from the blessing that is about to come to him or her.

Demonic signature: A certain young female undergraduate, who used to make a mockery of her lecturers who preached the gospel to her changed her music when she woke up one morning and found a signature on her palm. The signature was written in a strange language she did not understand. She used all kinds of soap to wash it away but it did not go. Eventually, she had to go to the preachers she had mocked for help. These lecturers preached to her and prayed that the evil signature should go off and it disappeared. That was an evil signature. She was lucky to have seen it physically. People who have evil signatures on their bodies do not prosper. Whatever they lay their hands on will not work. Marks of scratches that people see on their bodies when they wake up from sleep are evil signatures. They must be rubbed off.

Way Out

Clean off the marks and stamps by the blood of Jesus. Invite the Holy Ghost power to burn away the demonic pen used to write them.

Release yourself from any evil linkage. Psalm 97: 10 says, "Ye that love the Lord, hate evil: he preserveth the souls of his saints; he delivereth them out of the hand of the wicked." Psalm 149: 5-9 says, "Let the saints be joyful in glory. Let them sing aloud upon their beds. Let the high praises of God be in their mouth, and a two- edged sword in their hands. To execute vengeance upon the heathen and punishment upon the people. To bind their kings with chains, and their nobles with fetters of iron. To execute upon them the judgment written: This honor have all his saints. Praise ye the Lord." These scriptures give us the right to rewind or recall any evil that has been done to anyone in the past and to execute judgment on behalf of God. Colossians 2:14-15 says, "Blotting out the handwriting of ordinances that was against us, which was contrary to us, and took it out of the way, nailing it to his cross. And having spoiled principalities and powers, he made a show of them openly, triumphing over them in it." That is the stand of scripture. 1 John 3:8 says, "...For this purpose the Son of God was manifested, that he might destroy the works of the devil." You will be amazed at how many people the devil has tormented and is still tormenting with shadows. You must pray aggressively to defeat them because we know that they do not have the final say on your life. It is only God that has the final say but if you don't bring God into the situation, He will be watching you. If you bring Him in, you can take back what has been taken away from you by violence.

PRAYER POINTS
1. I refuse death and curses, in the name of Jesus.
2. I choose life and blessings, in Jesus' name.

3. I cancel all satanic claims against me, in the name of Jesus.
4. I shake off every strange touch, in the name of Jesus.
5. I bind the spirit of death and hell, in the name of Jesus.
6. Every strange call upon my life, go back to the sender, in the name of Jesus.
7. You snake spirit, I bruise your head, in the name of Jesus.
8. You demonic handwriting, I rub you off with the blood of Jesus, in Jesus' name.
9. (Place one hand on your head and the other one on your stomach as you take this prayer point) Holy Ghost fire, begin to burn in my body, in the name of Jesus.
10. I break every curse of blindness, in the name of Jesus.
11. Wonderful God, I thank you, in Jesus' name.

Chapter Eight

Inspirational Thoughts

The Old Mule

A parable is told of a farmer who owned an old mule. The mule fell into the farmer's well. The farmer heard the mule 'braying' – or whatever mules do when they fall into wells. After carefully assessing the situation, the farmer sympathized with the mule, but decided that neither the mule nor the well was worth the trouble of saving. Instead, he called his neighbors together and told them what had happened...and enlisted them to help haul dirt to bury the old mule in the well and put him out of his misery.

Initially, the old mule was hysterical! But as the farmer and his neighbors continued shoveling and the dirt hit his back...a thought struck him. It suddenly dawned on him that every time a shovel load of dirt landed on his back... HE SHOULD SHAKE IT OFF AND STEP UP!

This he did, blow after blow. "Shake it off and step up...shake it off and step up...shake it off and step up!" he repeated to encourage himself. No matter how painful the blows, or distressing the situation seemed the old mule fought "panic" and just kept right on SHAKING IT OFF AND STEPPING UP!

You're right! It wasn't long before the old mule, battered and exhausted, stepped triumphantly over the wall of that well! What seemed like it would bury him, actually blessed him...All because of the manner in which he handled his adversity.

Hebrews 12:1-2 says "Wherefore seeing we also are compassed about with so great a cloud of witnesses, let us lay aside every weight, and the sin which doth so easily beset us, and let us run with patience the race that is set before us, Looking unto Jesus the author and finisher of our faith; who for the joy that was set before him endured the cross, despising the shame, and is set down at the right hand of the throne of God."

Whether you will be buried or blessed depends on your own choice. Adversity, criticism and distraction can either bury you or bless you. It depends on your attitude towards them. The choice is yours. God bless you.

The Sand Box

A little boy was spending his Saturday morning playing in his sandbox. He had with him his box of cars and trucks, his plastic pail, and a shiny, red plastic shovel. In the process of creating roads and tunnels in the soft sand, he discovered a large rock in the middle of the sandbox.. The lad dug around the rock, managing to dislodge it from the dirt. With no little bit of struggle, he pushed and nudged the rock across the sandbox by using his feet. (He was a very small boy and the rock was very huge.) When the boy got the rock to the edge of the sandbox, however, he found that he couldn't roll it up and over the little wall..

Determined, the little boy shoved, pushed, and pried, but every time he thought he had made some progress, the rock tipped and then fell back into the sandbox.. The little boy grunted, struggled, pushed, shoved-but his only reward was to have the rock roll back, smashing his chubby fingers.. Finally he burst into tears of frustration... All this time the boy's father watched from his living room window as the drama unfolded.

At the moment the tears fell, a large shadow fell across the boy and the sandbox. It was the boy's father... Gently but firmly he said, "Son, why didn't you use all the strength that you had available?" Defeated, the boy sobbed back, "But I did, Daddy, I did! I used all the strength that I had! "No, son," corrected the father kindly. "You didn't use all the strength you had. You didn't ask me." With that the father reached down, picked up the rock, and removed it from the sandbox.

"Ask, and it shall be given you; seek, and ye shall find; knock, and it shall be opened unto you: For every one that asketh receiveth; and he that seeketh findeth; and to him that knocketh it shall be opened. Or what man is there of you, whom if his son ask bread, will he give him a stone? Or if he ask a fish, will he give him a serpent? If ye then, being evil, know how to give good gifts unto your children, how much more shall your Father which is in heaven give good things to them that ask him?" – Matthew 7:7-11

Effective Weapons

The most effective weapons of believers are the weapons of Love and Unity. Without these weapons we will be fighting a lost battle. During World War II, Hitler commanded all religious groups to unite so that he could control them. Among the Brethren assemblies, half complied and half refused. Those who went along with the order had a much easier time. Those who did not, faced harsh persecution. In almost every family of those who resisted, someone died in a concentration camp.

When war was over, feelings of bitterness ran deep between the groups and there was much tension. Finally they decided that the situation had to be healed. Leaders from each group met at a quiet retreat. For several days, each person spent time in prayer, examining his own heart in the light of Christ's commands. Then they came together. Francis Schaeffer, who told of the incident, asked a friend who was there, "What did you do then?" "We were just one," he replied. As they confessed their hostility and bitterness to God and yielded to His control, the Holy Spirit created a spirit of unity among them. Love filled their hearts and dissolved their hatred.

When love prevails among believers, especially in times of strong disagreement, it presents to the world an indisputable mark of a true follower of Jesus Christ.

Psalms 133:1-3 says "Behold, how good and how pleasant it is for brethren to dwell together in unity!... for there the LORD commanded the blessing, even life for evermore."

Snowflakes are one of nature's most fragile things, but just look at what they can do when they stick together. When we love one another with the love of God, we can face our common enemy, the devil. We will dwell together in unity and God will command His blessings upon us. This will make believers to come to the true knowledge of God. Think about it and till we meet again, stay blessed.

The Honeymoon is over

A young couple got married and left on their honeymoon. When they got back, the bride immediately called her Mother. "Well," said her Mother "so how was the honeymoon?"

"Oh, Mama," she replied, "the honeymoon was wonderful! So romantic..."Suddenly she burst out crying. "But, Mama, as soon as we returned Sam started using the most horrible language – things I'd never heard before I mean, all these awful 4-letter words! You've got to come get me and take me home…PLEASE Mama!"

"Sarah, Sarah," her Mother said, "calm down! Tell me, what could be so awful? WHAT 4-letter words?"

"Please don't make me tell you, Mama," wept the daughter, "I'm so embarrassed they're just too awful! COME GET ME, PLEASE!!!

"Darling, baby, you must tell me what makes you so upset… Tell your Mother the 4-letter words!" Still sobbing, the bride said, "Oh, Mama…words like: Dust, Wash, Iron, and Cook!

Sister, marriage is not about honeymoon, it is about taking covenant responsibilities.

Brother, "And the LORD God said, it is not good that the man should be alone; I will make him an help meet for him." She is an help meet and not a slave.

Marriage is like a business, the more you invest in it, the more valuable it becomes. "Two are better than one; because they have a good reward for their labour. For if they fall, the one will lift up his fellow: but woe to him that is alone when he falleth; for he hath not another to help him up. Again, if two lie together, then they have heat: but how can one be warm alone? Eccl 4:9-11

The Fence

There was a little boy with a bad temper. His father gave him a bag of nails and told him that every time he lost his temper, to hammer a nail in the back fence. The first day the boy had driven 37 nails into the fence. Then it gradually dwindled down. He discovered it was easier to hold his temper than to drive those nails into the fence. Finally the day came when the boy didn't lose his temper at all. He told his father about it and the father suggested that the boy now pull out one nail for each day that he was able to hold his temper.

The days passed and the young boy was finally able to tell his father that all the nails were gone. The father took his son by the hand and led him to the fence. He said, "You have done well, my son, but look at the holes in the fence. The fence will never be the same. When you say things in anger, they leave a scar just like this one. You can put a knife in a man and draw it out. It won't matter how many times you say I'm sorry, the wound is still there.

A verbal wound is as bad as a physical one. Friends are a very rare jewel, indeed. They make you smile and encourage you to succeed. They lend an ear, they share a word of praise, and they always want to open their hearts to us. Are you a friend? This is a challenge to you as a child of God.

Psalm 12:3 says "The Lord shall cut off all flattering lips, and the tongue that speaketh proud things."

Beloved, "Keep thy tongue from evil, and thy lips from speaking guile." Psalm 34:13.

God bless you.

Love

Show me a church where there is love, and I will show you a church that is a power in the community. In Chicago a few years ago a little boy attended a Sunday school I know of. When his parents moved to another part of the city the little fellow still attended the same Sunday school, although it meant a long, tiresome walk each way. A friend asked him why he went so far, and told him that there were plenty of others just as good nearer his home.

"They may be as good for others, but not for me," was his reply.

"Why not?" she asked.

"Because they love a fellow over there," he replied.

If only we could make the world believe that we loved them there would be fewer empty churches, and a smaller proportion of our population who never darken a church door. Let love replace duty in our church relations, and the world will soon be evangelized.

Chapter Nine

The Appointed Time

The topic of our message this week is entitled, "The appointed time." Job 14: 14 ; "If a man die, shall he live again? All the days of my appointed time will I wait, till my change come."

A bus-stop is usually an interesting place and full of activities. You find some people who come there sluggishly; they are not really in a hurry. Such people pick and choose the vehicle to board. Whereas you find some people struggling to catch any vehicle going their direction because they are already late. Sometimes in their rush, they enter the wrong bus. Some would prefer to take taxis in order to meet their appointments. It all has to do with timing.

It is a bad thing when you miss the appointed

time. Jesus said to the city of Jerusalem, "O Jerusalem, Jerusalem, thou that killest the prophets, and stonest them which are sent unto thee, how often would I have gathered thy children together, even as a hen gathereth her chickens under her wings, and would not! Behold, your house is left unto you desolate. For I say unto you, Ye shall not see me henceforth, till ye shall say, Blessed is he that cometh in the name of the Lord." (Matthew 23: 37 – 39).

Jesus told Jerusalem that her house would be left desolate because she did not know her time of visitation. The Messiah was promised and they refused to recognize Him. They decided that the best thing for the Messiah was to kill Him. This is the reason Jerusalem is still in trouble now. When the Jews came to Jesus and said, "Look at this beautiful temple. Isn't it wonderful?" Jesus said, "A time is coming when none of these stones shall stand on one another. They shall all be thrown down." They did not believe Him because the temple was solidly built and had gold and different kinds of ornament in it. Eventually, the word of Jesus came to pass. The temple with everything in it was destroyed, and now there is a mosque there. It is a bad thing when you miss the appointed time.

Time is an important part of our lives. All the popular questions that we ask ourselves about time, for example, how old are you? What is your experience? How long is this or that, etc, are not of interest to God. Rather the question He is interested in is, "What have you done?" To God, every purpose of His has a time. Isaiah 55: 8-9: "For my thoughts are not your thoughts, neither are your ways my ways, saith the Lord. For as the heavens are higher than the earth, so are my ways higher than your ways, and my thoughts than your thoughts." Verse 11 says, "So shall my word be that goeth forth out of my mouth: it shall not return unto me void, but it shall accomplish that which I please, and it shall prosper in the thing whereto I sent it." Sometimes when you are pestering God concerning a particular thing and He does not grant it immediately, it is because His ways are higher than your ways and He knows the best time to grant your request. At times when it seemed as if God was not moving, it was not that He was not concerned. It could be that the time was not yet right. When the mother of Jesus told the people at the marriage at Cana of Galilee to approach Him for wine, He said to her, "Woman, my hour has not come," and when His hour came, He said, "Father, this is the hour.

Glorify Yourself."

Beloved, one fact you must know is that if God is for you it does not matter who is against you. Anyone that is against you shall eat his flesh and drink his own blood. But if God is against you, no matter who your supporters are, they would be destroyed by fire. God has a purpose for making this message available to you. I believe that you are not reading it by chance but by the leading of the Holy Spirit.

It is a fruitless effort to bring your bucket out when the rain has stopped falling. Psalm 119: 126 says, "It is time for thee, Lord, to work: for they have made void thy law." I counsel you to confess this scripture seven times and to pray it aggressively because it is time for God to bless you. If it were not time for God to work in your life, you would not come across this message. Now is the appointed time Please pray the following prayer points:

Oh Lord, it is time for you to do a miracle in my life, in the name of Jesus.

All powers trying to keep my life stagnant be roasted, in Jesus' name.

The God we serve is very particular about time. One of the worst demons that Satan assigns to people is the one that slows them down so that they never do anything on time. This demon is called the spirit of the tail. It is a powerful demon that we must watch out for. God will never come late into any situation. What we are saying is that miracles may not come at your own time but God will not come late. Many times in our lives, we try to time God forgetting that He has His own timing. People may be mocking you now that you are running about and carrying Bible but one thing is sure: the answer to your prayers will not come late. Good change will not come late. Your favourable situations will not come late.

When we fulfill our own part, God will certainly visit us. For example, we start our program on Sundays at 10.00 a.m., Mondays at 6.30 p.m. and on Wednesdays at 6.00 p.m. All these periods are already written down in God's book. So, immediately we get close to these periods, there are special angels who are around to record the names of the early risers, that is, those who come on time, and once the service starts they take off. So, God is particular about time. If God says we should meet at 7 a.m. and you get there at 7.30 a.m. you better apologize because with God,7 is 7. Some people come when the angels have gone. You, as a child of God, must do all things on time. Ecclesiastes 3: 1-8:

"To everything there is a season, and a time to every purpose under the heaven: A time to be born, and a time to die; a time to plant, and a time to pluck up that which is planted. A time to kill, and a time to heal. A time to break down, and a time to build up. A time to weep, and a time to laugh; a time to mourn, and a time to dance. A time to cast away stones, and a time to gather stones together; a time to embrace, and a time to refrain from embracing. A time to get, and a time to lose; a time to keep, and a time to cast away. A time to rend, and a time to sew; a time to keep silence, and a time to speak. A time to love, and a time to hate; a time of war, and a time of peace."

Everything in the plan of God has been timed. Your miracle has its own appointed time. When Joseph was in the prison, he interpreted the dreams of the chief butler and the chief baker. According to his interpretation, the butler's dream meant that he would be restored to his job while the one of the baker meant that he would be killed. The butler was happy and promised to tell the king about Joseph when he is restored. But the Bible says that when the chief butler got to the king's palace, he forgot all about Joseph. Why did he forget? God caused him to forget because that time was not

God's appointed time for Joseph. Two years after the man had forgotten him, God Himself brought him out. God has a time-table for your life. John the Baptist was to be six months older than Jesus Christ. It was God's time. We are discussing this today because the Lord said your time has come. The children of Israel were in bondage for 430 years but when it was God's time to bring them out, it took Him only one night. The birth and crucifixion of our Lord Jesus Christ were all according to God's time-table.

Failure to move when God is moving is very disastrous. Failure to pray hard when prayer points are called and others are praying hard could be disastrous. On their way to the Promised Land, the children of Israel decided to move outside of God's timing, they ended with defeat. If God moves and leaves you behind, you need to cry for mercy. It is the high time to come to the camp of holiness, purity, power, prosperity and healing. If God asks you to witness to a person and you refuse to and the person dies, you will be in trouble because you have missed His time. It is very dangerous to take a short cut when you are dealing with God. Please, pray this prayer point: "I reject every sin of taking a short cut, in the name of Jesus."

What is the meaning of taking a short cut?

Before they had Isaac, Abraham and Sarah decided to take a short cut. The short cut brought about somebody called Ishmael. It was the wife of Abraham that pushed Abraham into it. We know what Ishmael has done to the whole world now. Two generations later, the family of Abraham had another person who was like Ishmael. His name was Dan. When Rachael pushed Jacob to Leah, Leah gave birth to Dan. In the book of Revelation when God began to list the 12 children of Israel, He removed this Dan and replaced him with Joseph's son called Manasseh. That is what happens when a short cut is taken. God has His own program for every life; that is why you must not use other people's lives as a yardstick to measure yours. God's program for us may look alike but they are different. Your personal program for your life may lead you to failure and destruction if it is not in line with God's program for you.

God's program and time may look unattractive but they are the best. Many of us need to correct our ideas about God. The God who rained manna from heaven for the children of Israel was the same God who rained fire and brimstone on Sodom and Gomorrah. The God who called Moses was the same God who prevented him from entering the Promised Land. The Lord God that made Saul a king was the same God that dethroned him. The Lord God that healed Namaan was the same God that transferred his leprosy to Gehazi. The God that blessed David and made him to become king in Israel was the same God who put curses on him. The God that gave Samson power was the same God who allowed his eyes to be removed and to be punished. The God that made Zechariah to serve in the temple was the same God who allowed him to be rendered dumb. With God there is no middle camp. God is a God of joy, love, peace, miracles and power but you must also remember that He is a God of righteousness and judgment.

Many years ago, I taught Biology in an Adult Education school. I had about 120 students in my class. The first thing I taught them was living and non-living things. I told them about the amoeba. After I made some explanations, I asked them if they understood the lesson and they said, "No." I repeated the lesson two more times and asked if they now understood it. One man stood up and said, "Where is the wife of amoeba?" I felt frustrated but explained to him that it was not necessary for amoeba to marry. What was the problem with them?

Timing. They were doing the right thing at the wrong time. You could do the right thing at the wrong time or the wrong thing at the right time. They are both the same thing – wrong timing. When you change your position, God too changes your situation. It is that change that is so difficult for most of us.

After service some time ago, a man came to me for counseling and said, "What a wonderful fellowship. I know that the church I attend now is bad but when I get there, everybody stands at attention and greets me. So, I may find it difficult to continue to come here because in this place, nobody can hail me. Nobody recognizes anybody. I cannot bear it. I prefer a place where I am known and recognized." When I discussed further with him, I discovered that he did not know anything about the Holy Spirit and did not believe in the teachings of Apostle Paul. I could see that he was bent on his opinions. He was refusing to change his position so God could not change his situation. What will kill most people is their various church posts. The devil has used these to stagnate many lives. I have a friend who before he became a pastor was a priest somewhere. As a priest, during communion, he used to lust after the girls who came for the communion service and each time he sat at the altar, something would be saying to him: "Can't you see that you are not saved? You would perish if care is not taken." He struggled with this for some time until one day, he decided to give his life to the Lord and became a floor member of a Pentecostal church. Not long after he gave his life to Christ, God began to promote him. If he was bent on remaining a priest in his former church, wearing cassocks and carrying a big bag about, God would not have changed his situation. If you cry for a change, God too will cry for repentance. Once He cries for repentance and you repent, the change comes. From time immemorial prophets of God had always cried that people should repent and make a turn around. The Bible says, "If my people which are called by my name, shall humble themselves, and pray and seek my face and turn from their wicked ways, then I too will perform" (2 Chronicles 7: 14). God says He would perform once we do our own part. You are the pointer towards what God wants to do in your life. You may be wondering why the heavens seem so closed to you now and nothing is coming through. All that God is saying is, "Change." He is an orderly God. He will not put the cart before the horse. If you need to obtain certain things or meet a certain standard before He gives something to you, He will not give it to you until you change. For some people, God is only waiting for them to remove anger from their lives, then the power they are calling for so much will come upon them. God will not give you power when He knows that you will misuse it.

A lot of people are praying that God should bless them with money when they are still very covetous. The blessing will not come until that covetousness goes. Some people are busy revealing their secrets to their enemies and God wants to teach them how to shut their mouths before He gives them their miracles so that they will not spoil their miracles with their own mouths. God is ready when we are ready. Unfortunately, today, there are people who want to run faster than God. Some even try to know better than God. Many people lack patience and are in a hurry. Isaiah 28: 16: "Therefore thus saith the Lord God, Behold, I lay in Zion for a foundation a stone, a tried stone, a precious corner, a sure foundation; he that believeth shall not make haste." That is, you will not be in a hurry. The Bible says, "Of all my appointed time, I will wait till my changes come."

Patience is one of the greatest virtues that

God gave to man. Impatience has destroyed so many things, lives, homes, families and nations. Some people keep crying day and night that they must get married and God is saying to them: "Be patient. Your partner is on the way." Some will say, "If God does not move fast enough, I will go back to my former boyfriend because no Christian has proposed marriage to me." Others are saying, "I must get rich now." And God is saying, "Prosperity is on the way, be patient." A certain woman kept crying that she wanted to get rich. She gathered some money and planned to travel to England. Her poor husband escorted her to the airport and after they said farewell, he waited at the airport to have a drink before he went home. Suddenly, he heard his name over the microphone that his attention was needed at the information desk if he was still around. Immediately he got there, policemen held his hand and led him inside and behold, he saw that his wife had been arrested. What happened? She tried to smuggle out cocaine. When her husband found out what happened, he fainted. Impatience had caused a lot of problems for many people. Many people have gone back to square one because of impatience. These things are so important that the Bible says so much about them. Three important principles must be clear to us before we start praying.

There is time for everything. Doing things at the wrong time would lead to disaster.

God Himself has appointed a time for your miracle. Has God assured you through prophecies, dreams and visions about a thing? Then wait for the appointed time. Don't go and try the enemy's camp.

3. Patience is a great virtue.

If you study the history of Science, you would find out that the inventors of most of the things we are enjoying now were first of all ridiculed. People laughed at them but they remained patient and continued with their works. When the first men that made motor cars were working on their cars, people abused them in the streets and told them to go and buy horses instead of wasting their time on the dirty thing they call motor cars. It was the same with those who invented the telephone and the Aero plane. Those were men of the world who did not know the Bible. You need to see what the Bible says about patience. Lack of patience robbed Saul of his kingdom. If he had waited a little bit for Samuel to arrive there would have been no problem. A few minutes of impatience caused Moses the Promised Land. We need to pray that divine patience should come upon us so that we can wait for God's timing and not wanting Him to work with our own time. We need patience for the word of God to bear fruit in our lives. We need patience too to possess our possessions. The school of patience brings you hope. By faith and patience, promises are inherited.

In His word, our Lord promised us healing. But this healing would not come instantly on everybody. Some will recover instantly while others will recover gradually. But when you are not patient, you may miss it. You need patience to run the Christian race. The Bible says that we should run with patience the race ahead of us. Patience too, is a sign of Christian maturity. An impatient believer is a baby Christian. Patience receives answers to prayers. This is one of the secrets behind the success of the Psalmist. We must cultivate it.

Many People Are Impatient For The Following Reasons:

Lack of brotherly love.

Spirit of competition.

Pride.

Stubbornness.

The Bible does not want us to be impatient because when God decides that it is your time, everything will cooperate with you. People who are against you will start working for you. Even those who do not like you will become your friends.

Please, be aggressive in your prayers. God bless you as you do so, in Jesus' name.

PRAYER POINTS

1. Oh Lord, don't ever leave me behind. Let me be going with You all the time, in the name of Jesus.
2. Oh Lord, let me be in the right place at the right time, in the name of Jesus.
3. Oh Lord, restore to me everything I have lost through impatience, in the name of Jesus.
4. It is time for You, O Lord, to turn my life to miracles, in the name of Jesus.
5. I refuse to waste my life. I refuse to waste my time, in the name of Jesus.
6. Oh Lord, Your purpose for bringing this message to me will not be defeated in my life, in Jesus' name.
7. I refuse to labor in vain, in the name of Jesus.
8. Let household wickedness be put to flight,

in the name of Jesus.

9. Let all anti-glory forces lose their hold upon my life, in the name of Jesus.
10. I release myself from the bondage of leaking pockets, in the name of Jesus.
11. Father Lord, give me supernatural breakthroughs in all my endeavors, in the name of Jesus.
12. I bind and put to flight all the spirits of fear, anxiety and discouragement, in Jesus' name.
13. Lord, show me dreams and visions that would advance my cause, in the name of Jesus.
14. Lord, let your divine patience come upon my life, in Jesus' name.

www.ingramcontent.com/pod-product-compliance
Lightning Source LLC
Chambersburg PA
CBHW072124170626
46813CB00004B/1682